Inspector
West
Takes Charge

SUPERINTENDENT WEST STORIES

by John Creasey

Inspector West Takes Charge

JOHN CREASEY

Charles Scribner's Sons

New York

First American Edition 1972

A-8.72 (C)

Printed in the United States of America
Library of Congress Catalog Card Number 72-1189
SBN 684-13007-6

1

THE KITTEN

The kitten rubbed against Roger West's legs in the darkness, making him jump and switch on his torch. In the light two large eyes glowed. Then the kitten stretched, and disappeared.

Roger continued his brisk walk, heels ringing on the pavement, until the white blur of a painted gatepost showed in starlit darkness. He turned into the gateway, taking out his keys and inserting one by sense of touch. He stepped into the dark hall, kicked against something which shouldn't be there, and went sprawling.

The torch shot from his hand and fell on the carpet, the keys rattled, and as he flung out his hand to save himself he touched the top of an umbrella stand. That crashed, too.

A stream of light came from a door on the right of the small, square hall. Outlined against it was a woman with disheveled hair. She wore a dark blue dressing-gown which covered her feet except for the points of red slippers. She stared at Roger accusingly.

"Hallo, darling," he said. "Not in bed?"

"Just as well," said "darling." "What have you been up to?"

Roger stood up gingerly.

"I think I've brought you a present," he replied.

"So I should think. It's a quarter to one. Where is it?"

"That's what I'm wondering," sighed Roger, peering about the semi-darkness. "What's that just behind you?"

His wife refused to look behind her.

"I knew you had all the other faults but I thought you could hold your beer," she said. "Stop joking." Then suddenly she swung round. "Something touched my leg, I know it did!"

"I warned you," said Roger. "I know it touched mine, and I feared it meant trouble. Keep quite still, now, don't move." He pulled the skirt of the dressing-gown up slowly, and a dark grey shape flew towards a chair. A plaintive *miaow* followed.

"A cat!" exclaimed Janet West. "Why on earth did you bring a cat home?"

"Kitten," corrected Roger. "And it brought me. Puss, puss! Come and let's have a look at you." He bent down on one knee and peered beneath the chair. "Scared out of its life," he remarked, standing up. "What happens now? A saucer of milk?"

"We've hardly got enough for morning tea."

"We could open a tin. Sweetheart, did I tell you that you have the most adorable nose?"

"Did I ever tell you that you have the most deplorable nerve?" Janet looked round at the sound of another *miaow*. "I wouldn't mind a cup of tea," she admitted.

Roger filled the kettle while Janet poured milk into a saucer and put it as near the kitten's nose as the ball of fur would permit. It examined the milk suspiciously, and began to lap.

"It's famished," declared Roger.

Janet carried the tea tray into the lounge, where a few embers glowed in a tiled grate. The kitten followed, arching its back, then curling itself into a ball near the fire.

"The kitten at home," remarked Roger. "What shall we call it?"

"I don't say I wouldn't like a kitten," Janet admitted, pouring tea, "but someone will come looking for it in the morning. Did you really fall over it?"

"Certainly not," said Roger. "I was drunk. My wife told me so. Ah, a cup of tea's good. I had a snack at Mark's," he went on, "but that was just after seven. We got stuck into this blasted Prendergast job then, and I didn't realize it was so late."

"Before long I'm going to rule bachelor friends off your calling list," said Janet. "Mark can go to bed and get up when he wants to, but you haven't time to spend chasing after imaginary crimes. I wish Mark had never put the idea into your head. Why shouldn't three people die in the same family within six months? Just because you don't like Prendergast's taste in trousers that doesn't make him a triple murderer. Only you and Mark ever think about it, and if the whole of Scotland Yard is satisfied I don't see why its youngest Chief Inspector shouldn't be."

"All of Scotland Yard except me?" mused Roger. "I wonder. What it is to be a policeman!" He eyed the kitten thoughtfully, and lit a cigarette. "You're right in one thing, sweet, I don't like Claude Prendergast's trousers, and his wife is too overpowering. Now they've inherited the money she'll start buying sables, and he'll invest in a Rolls-Royce."

"You're much too bright for one o'clock in the morning," said Janet, stifling a yawn. "I must go to bed."

"Shut that creature in the kitchen first," Roger urged.

When Janet had gone, he leaned forward and stirred the embers, wooing a lick of flame. The Prendergast business was becoming an obsession, perhaps. Every time it began to fade, Mark Lessing gave it life and colour. Confound the Prendergasts!

Mrs. Prendergast made two of her husband in size, and gave him no chance to wear the trousers, but flamboyancy and ghoulish enjoyment did not make her a murderess. Few would give either Claude or Maisie Prendergast—what a name for that female mountain!—credit for cold-blooded murder; or rather, three cold-blooded murders. If credit was the proper word.

Mark was right in one respect. It had been a peculiar series of accidents. First there was Septimus, drowned in his swimming pool with only the vaguest suggestion of a bruise on the back of his head, no real evidence that he had been struck. Sibley, the

Home Office pathologist, refused to say that violence had been used, and the verdict at the inquest had been *death by misadventure*.

Septimus Prendergast's fortune, nearly a million pounds, even after the death duties had done their damnedest, had been enjoyed by his son Monty for only three weeks. Then Monty had fallen over the edge of a cliff in Cornwall. No one knew why he had been in Cornwall, but everyone knew that he would not walk along a cliff on a bleak winter's morning out of *joie de vivre* or a desire to slim. There had been no evidence of foul play, however. *Death by misadventure* again, and death duties took a few more hundred thousands from the Prendergast fortune before Waverley Prendergast inherited. Waverley had been knocked down by a car, the driver of which did not stop. *Death by misadventure*, after police SOS calls over the radio had brought no response.

Claude Prendergast was the only known surviving relative. After death duties had hit the jackpot again, Claude took over something like four hundred thousand pounds, Delaware, the Surrey house, and 48 Braddon Square, the London house. Not to mention the business worth at least thirty thousand a year. In six months Claude had jumped from an allowance of two thousand a year, more than his father had really considered him worth, to a capital of four hundred thousand pounds plus the shares, and thus profits from Prendergast, Blight & Company Limited, far better known as the proprietors of *Dreem* cigarettes and *Dreem* tobacco.

Dreem, the tobacco of your dreams! cooed the commercials. No one stood to inherit after Claude, and there was a condition in the original will, Septimus's will, which left the money to charities if it passed out of the family. Not one or two large charities, but seventy-four, no single one being allotted more than 3 per cent of the final residue. No motive there, even if a reasoning and logical member of the C.I.D. ever allowed himself to think that the executive of any charity would commit murder for the profit of a charitable organization. No one had had a motive except Claude and Maisie. The *Dreem* shares were blameless, too; they had to go on the open market.

"There's one possibility outside Claude and Maisie," Mark Lessing had said earlier that evening. "Someone might want to break up the company. But Maisie is clever behind that purple exterior of hers, she knew what was coming. Depend on it, she will have the money settled on her in the next few months, and then off will pop little Claude. We can't stop a settlement, we don't even know what lawyer she will use."

"If we knew the lawyer we couldn't stop anything," Roger had retorted. "I've learned one thing you'll love. Maisie and Claude have been to see Gabby Potter several times."

"*That* old scoundrel!" Mark's excitement had risen sky high. "There's your chance! Dig up a reason for a search warrant, and find what Potter's had to do with the Prendergasts."

"What do you think I'm looking for? The sack?"

"If I were at the Yard I'd have Potter in jug in five minutes. He's the biggest crook in England, and should have been in Dartmoor years ago."

"There are other prisons than Dartmoor," Roger had pointed out.

Now, with Janet upstairs, waiting, Roger smoothed his pipe and tried to get the Prendergasts out of his mind. The thought of Potter handling any part of the Prendergast business was disturbing, but the idea that Maisie Prendergast, *née* Webb, had married Claude because he might eventually inherit the *Dreem* fortune was simply a guess. Whatever Mark said, Maisie hadn't the mental equipment required. But supposing someone wanted control of the *Dreem* company through Claude, and planned to use Maisie as his instrument? Gabby Potter was exactly the man to handle dubious company work; many company promoters who side-stepped the law were amongst his clients.

The telephone was on a table behind him. He reached for it and dialled Mark's Chelsea number. The Wests lived in Fulham, not twenty minutes walk away from Mark's bachelor flat.

The ringing sound continued in his ears for more than a minute. He put the receiver down and dialled again, but only the burr-burr rewarded him, yet he knew there was a telephone next to Mark's bed.

. . . .

P. C. Diver, of the Division in which Mark Lessing lived, knew that Lessing was a friend of West of the Yard, and kept a benevolent eye on Lessing's home. He knew, also, that Lessing was regarded by the Yard as a shrewd amateur. Diver had little time for amateurs, and the word *criminologist* never impressed him, but he knew Lessing fairly well, and liked him.

He was puzzled when he saw the little car standing outside the block of flats where Lessing lived, because it was in the early hours, and the last time he had passed there had been no car there. Tenants always took theirs to the underground car park. True, there was nothing surprising in the situation itself; a resident could have been brought home by a friend. Friends of the residents of this particular block of luxury flats, however, seldom drove around in dilapidated pre-war Fords. This one looked much the worse for wear. Pondering over all this, Diver asked himself whether there was any possibility of a burglar. The thought half-scared and half-excited him. He considered hurrying away and telephoning the station, but if it was a false alarm he would look a proper Charley.

He decided to wait by the car and have a word with whoever came to claim it; if it was a man carrying a bag or a case, then he—P. C. Diver—might pull off a single-handed capture which would bring kudos and might help towards promotion. His curiosity grew sharper, and he decided to walk towards the entrance of the flats to see if there were any obvious signs of trouble.

As he stepped inside, not exactly nervous but a little on edge, he did not see the man crouching behind the massive front door.

He heard a whisper of movement, swung round, and saw a man jumping at him. The man's arm was upraised, and he held a weapon. Diver flung himself backwards. The weapon caught his shoulder, and sent him staggering, and he tripped over a rug. As he crashed down, he tried to pull his whistle from his pocket, but fumbled it. Alarm rose to screaming point, until he saw the man racing out of the entrance hall. He tried to scramble to his feet, but kept slipping. By the time he reached the street doorway, the old Ford was moving off and all Diver could see was the silhouette of the man's head and shoulders at the driving window.

Diver wasted no more time. Hugging his shoulder and limping from a bruised knee, he stumbled across to the caretaker's flat, woke the man, and telephoned the division.

"The first place I'd try, sir," he said to the inspector who came at the double, "is Mr. Lessing's. You know, Chief Inspector West's friend." Under his breath, he added: "That swine would have smashed my head in. God knows what he's done to Lessing."

2

QUICK LOOK ROUND

Mark Lessing was lying on his stomach. Through the sheet wound tightly about his head he could hear the ringing of the telephone clearly, but there was no other sound audible, not a single movement from the men in the next room. It was possible that they had gone without letting him know. He eased his position, but there was no chance of answering the call. The devils had tied him to the bed too securely. At least they hadn't smashed his head in.

The telephone stopped, and he heard the sound of a drawer being opened; it was the middle drawer of the sideboard, which stuck and squeaked whenever it was moved in or out.

Silence followed, and seemed interminable. Had they gone? A sharp ring came, farther away than the telephone; the front door bell.

Whispered voices reached his ears, more stealthy sounds followed by the ring of his door bell. He thought he heard a door close, and made frantic efforts to move, succeeding only in making the cords at his wrists and ankles more uncomfortable. He heard nothing more until a sharp voice exclaimed:

"Well I'm damned!"

He did not recognize the voice, but he heard a door slam loudly enough to shake the bed and the pictures on the walls. Heavy footsteps sounded, followed by a confusion of sounds.

Then this door burst open, and a man exclaimed:

"Good God!"

"So Diver was right," another man said as he crossed swiftly. "Are you hurt, Mr. Lessing?"

.   .   .   .

"Your friend is all right," the Divisional Inspector assured Roger and Janet. "In fact he's sitting up and taking nourishment. Two men broke in and knocked him out and tied him to his bed. Then they searched the place. Turned it upside down in fact,—I don't know what he'll say when he sees it."

The door of the bedroom opened.

"You'll soon find out," Lessing said, and glared at Roger, then spotted Janet. "And *you?*" He pulled his dressing-gown together hurriedly. "Support me," he went on. "I bought a piece of Sèvres yesterday, so fragile that a puff of wind would break it. I hope—"

He broke off, in front of the living-room door. The sight which met his eyes silenced him. Roger frowned. Janet felt nauseated. A beautiful room had been ransacked, and nothing was in its right place.

Suddenly Lessing's face lit up.

"The vandals missed it," he said, and stepped to a cabinet, opened the glass door, and took out a beautiful figurine in pale pinks and blues. "Isn't she lovely?" he crooned.

The Divisional men looked faintly derisive.

Janet exclaimed: "It's beautiful!"

"Apart from china, what have you got that's worth stealing?" demanded Roger.

"One half-finished manuscript explaining why the police always get their man," said Mark. "It's in the study. I suppose they got that far." He led Roger to a door leading off the big room, and stopped short. "They certainly did."

The study was small, with three walls lined with bookcases, the fourth behind a large leather-topped desk. A Mirzapore carpet and three hide armchairs set off several pieces of richly-coloured china which stood on wall brackets. Only the china had been left untouched. The books had been tumbled from the shelves, the rest were lying on their sides. The chairs had been overturned and the webbing ripped apart. Every drawer in the desk was out, papers from them littered it and the floor.

Janet, peering over their shoulders and hugging the figurine, said:

"I should think they wanted to find something."

"I can't stand that kind of humour just now," Lessing protested. "It will take a week to put this room straight. And look at the manuscript!" Pages were all over the place, but none was torn. "The oafs, they've trodden on some." He bent down to pick up some sheets of paper covered with closely-written matter, while Roger looked about the room, examining the drawers of the desk closely.

He straightened up.

"Two locks forced by a man who knows his job," he declared. "This wasn't a burglary by chance, they were after something specific. I wonder who's out and could do this job," he added, as he looked down at the desk. "I saw Charlie Clay last week. Abie Fenton—but we won't get anywhere that way." He watched as Divisional men came in to check for fingerprints and other clues. Large men moved about the study soft-footed and gentle.

Better leave them to it, Roger thought, and went with Mark and Janet into the living room, where the police had finished.

"Might as well have a drink," Mark said. "Give that fire a poke, Jan." The fire was a dull reddish glow, but sparks flew when Janet thrust with the poker.

"Nothing for me," she said.

"Don't take too much whisky or your head will ache even more," Roger said.

"Your head's all right, I presume," Mark said sarcastically. He poured out. "What brought you?"

"A cat."

"Kitten," corrected Janet. "And a tom-cat who came home late."

"What?"

Janet explained.

"What brought the burglars is more to the point," Roger said. "One was seen to go, after clouting a local copper who had his suspicions about a car parked outside. There were two men here, you say?"

"Yes."

"Did they say what they wanted?"

"No."

"Any idea what it was?"

"Not the faintest."

"You've made yourself thoroughly unpopular with Prendergast and his Maisie," Roger remarked. "All the world knows that you think you have a peculiar prescience about crime, particularly murder, and you will insist on making your suspicions known."

"You've never known Mark get his teeth into a case without there being some cause," Janet interrupted. "And you know that he's been attacked before for poking his nose in."

"There's no obvious connexion between the burglary and the Prendergast affair suspicions," said Roger. "We don't even know that Mark knows anything that the imaginary murderer of the Prendergasts might want."

"Had you found anything, Mark?" asked Janet.

Lessing rubbed his nose.

"Nothing specific, but I talked too much in a television interview and hinted that I knew a lot."

"You'll get yourself in dock for slander."

"Not a hope. I've ideas, mind you, thousands of ideas floating about like clouds of ectoplasm and I put them all down on paper. I left the notes in the right-hand top drawer of my study desk. My God, do you think—"

They moved together. The police had finished in the study, but the top right-hand drawer of the desk was wide open. The contents had been emptied on to the floor. Roger rummaged through them, picking up a sheaf of papers covered with Mark's meticulous handwriting. The top sheet was headed: *"Death by Misadventure?"*

"It's all there," Mark confirmed, a minute or two later. "So they didn't come for that. No connexion with the Prendergast virtuoso proved."

"Don't misuse big words," said Janet.

"No misuse, sweetie. Murder is a fine art, and three Prendergasts have been murdered. I'm assuming the killer in each case was the same man, woman, or spirit. I had this beautifully-written treatise on the case in that drawer, and my visitors could have read it. The fact that they might have deliberately left the notes behind doesn't prove anything. Could the Prendergasts' killer have lost something he's anxious to get back, I wonder?"

"Have you stolen anything?" demanded Roger.

"No. But the P.K. might think I have—if he's lost anything of significance."

"Sheer guesswork," Roger protested, stifling a yawn. "We'll leave a man on duty outside your door, so that you can have a good sleep without being afraid."

"I'm not afraid," Mark declared. "I just want a few hours' rest."

"That's good," said Roger. "Then you'll be fit enough to call on Gabby Potter in the morning. If you do, you could make it obvious you connect him with this burglary. You might get an interesting reaction."

"Oh, no!" Janet cried.

"Damned good idea," enthused Lessing. "He knows I'm Prendergast case crazy. If he has any nefarious designs on the Prendergast money, we'll find out."

"Do you really think he's right?" Janet asked Roger, as they drove home.

"If Potter's involved or the Prendergasts have been murdered, Mark's stirring up mud which needs stirring. If he scares anyone they might get careless. That's Mark's real motivation, of course—he can do what the Yard can't. But don't ask me whether I think he's right about Potter."

. . . .

At the time when Roger and Janet were driving home, Mr. Gabriel Potter, Solicitor & Commissioner for Oaths, was sitting up in a four-poster bed in a large, high-ceilinged room in a very large house on the outskirts of London, and listening in to the telephone. A man with a gruff voice was saying:

"Not a thing there, Guv'nor. There wasn't nothing about you, neither. I saw the bit he'd written about Prendergast, though. Guesswork, that's all. I took a photo of each page, nearly got nabbed staying so long. I'll send the film over in the morning. The other stuff just wasn't there. I don't make mistakes like *that*."

"I trust not," said Potter. He was a thin man in feature, figure and voice. "I would like that film as soon as possible, please. Goodnight."

He replaced the receiver, put out the light and slid down in the bed, but he did not get to sleep at once. Potter's nights were usually so serene and untroubled; tonight he was preoccupied and uneasy.

When at last he did get to sleep, Claude Prendergast was blinking in a darkened room some miles away. He was restless because of a noise he could not get accustomed to; his wife's heavy breathing in the next bed. Now and again she raised her voice clearly in coherent speech. It was strange and to Claude a little improper to have a woman sleeping in the same room. Thought and contemplation of Maisie did not comfort Claude; he did not fully understand how he had come to marry her, but he had not yet reached the stage of wishing that he had resisted.

Quite loudly she said: "I wonder if he found them? I wonder if he found them?"

Then she heaved her flabby body over, and fell silent.

3

PHOTOGRAPHS AND THINGS

Janet West awakened first, stirred, stretched, and snuggled down to look at Roger's profile. He was on his back, with his lips closed, and was absurdly good-looking. There had been a time when she had doubted whether good looks could go with good sense, a keen brain, and the more attractive human traits. In Roger they did. If there was anything the matter with him it was that he took his work too seriously. Occasionally, he was inclined to take Mark too seriously, also.

"And yet, they scare me at times," admitted Janet. "What does Mark call it? . . . prescience. Last night, for instance. What made Roger decide to go over to his place?" In a louder voice she demanded: "Do you know anything you haven't told me?"

"Er," said Roger. "Wa' time?"

"Half-past ten," answered Janet, pushing the sheet back and taking a hold on his left ear. "Roger, why did you go to Mark's last night? What are you keeping from me?"

"Er," grunted Roger, and widened his eyes. "Ten? Half-past *ten?* Good Lord!" He flung the clothes back and jumped out of bed, then caught a glimpse of the clock on the dressing-table. He slumped down. "It's not much past eight."

From downstairs came a faint but distinctive *miaow*.

"Of course, we've got visitors," went on Roger, pulling on a dressing gown. "I'll make the tea, you lie in for a few minutes."

By the time he had brushed his teeth, the kettle was boiling.

He made the tea, then found Janet doing her hair in front of the mirror. He liked to watch her fingers twisting and turning in the curls at the nape of her neck. He liked what the movement of her arms above her head did to her figure, too.

He poured out the tea, and Janet asked:

"Do you know anything about the Prendergast business that I don't?"

"Nothing I can tell you," answered Roger. "Nothing I've told Mark, either. If you're really wondering why I went over to Chelsea, I just felt uneasy."

"Do you think Mark's in any danger?"

"Good Lord, no! If he had been we wouldn't have found him tied up last night, he would have been ready for a *post mortem*. It's puzzling though. I don't think he's working on anything but the Prendergast affair, the odds are that its connected with that. If it is——"

"Then it's a murder investigation."

"Multiple murder," Roger agreed. "Well, I must be off."

He planted a kiss on her forehead, promised to be home by half-past seven, turned away and tripped over the kitten. He saved himself from falling completely, while the kitten darted off, squawking.

"Poor little thing!" cried Janet.

"You might try to find its owner," said Roger bitterly. "If it's still around tonight, don't let it out of the kitchen until I get in. I don't feel safe opening a door."

Half-a-dozen uniformed men at the gates, in the hall and along the passages of New Scotland Yard wished Inspector West good morning. In the office which he shared with four other Detective Inspectors a sergeant was talking to a big, fat man at the next desk to Roger's. The fat man was Eddie Day, whose special subject was forgery.

"Hallo, hallo," said Day, in an unexpected falsetto and with a slight over-emphasis on the aitches. "How's Handsome Harry?"

The sergeant smiled dutifully.

"I took over from Sergeant Sloane, sir. He said you'd want to see these as soon as you were in. They're the fingerprints found at Mr. Lessing's flat." "These" were a sheaf of buff-coloured forms which he handed over; two white ones were on the top.

The white sheets were decorated with grey fingerprints. Roger eyed them without enthusiasm.

The sergeant went on: "One of them might be Charlie Clay's. There's just enough to line it up, but not strong enough to do anything. We know Clay's free."

"Are you looking for him?"

"He'll be brought in for questioning if you give the say-so."

"I say so," said Roger. "Nothing else?"

"Nothing of any use, sir."

Roger nodded, the sergeant went out, and Eddie Day breathed wheezily over a file of papers.

There was no trace of the car which had driven off from Mark's place the night before. Only one set of prints had been found. The opening of the drawers had certainly been the work of experts. Charlie Clay, Abie Fenton, and three or four other cracksmen known to be in London were named as possibles. Clay would probably prove the right man, if they could break the alibi he would doubtless have ready. Clay had a peculiarity common to no other cracksman. He always took off his gloves some time during a job, and three times had been "sent up" on the evidence of fingerprints he need not have made.

Roger considered what he knew of Clay. A big man who spoke in a thick, gruff voice, whom it was always difficult to identify. There was a vagueness about Charlie's personality which helped him considerably. The head and shoulders description given by P. C. Diver might or might not fit Clay.

Roger put the papers aside and went to a green filing cabinet, opening a drawer containing the "C"s and pulling out a stiff folder. A brief summary of Charlie Clay's dossier was there; one note said: *"Solicitors at last trial: Gabriel Potter & Son."*

Roger said: "I thought so."

"Why don't you keep quiet?" implored Eddie Day, looking up from two bank-notes which he was examining through a watch-maker's glass. "How do you expect me to concentrate?"

"I don't," said Roger. "Where are you going today?"

"Old Bailey," said Eddie. "And you?"

"Marlborough Street," said Roger. "A remand in custody, I hope."

At Marlborough Street he spent two hours in an oak-panelled court-room while the preliminary evidence against one Joseph Wright was taken. It was an unsavoury case; Wright was being charged with living on the immoral earnings of women. Roger found his mind only half on the evidence he heard and had to give. He was thinking of Gabriel Potter and Mark Lessing and wondering whether Mark had gone to see the solicitor?

. . . .

The office of Gabriel Potter was large, untidy, and dusty; Potter himself was as neat as he was thin. He was a solicitor who believed that the older and mustier his office the more reassuring it was to his clients. He sat at a roll-top desk poring over the photostat copies of Mark's *"Death by Misadventure?"* unsmiling, occasionally twitching his nostrils. The telephone, which served as a paperweight, rang sharply.

"Yes?" said Potter.

"There is a Mr. Lessing to see you, sir," said a girl in a piping treble. "Mr. Mark Lessing."

"Ask him to wait," said Potter. He frowned, replaced the receiver, and continued to read Mark's report on the Prendergast deaths. Finished, he folded the copies up and tucked them in an envelope. He put them into a pigeon-hole in the desk, without any attempt at concealment, and pressed a bell. He could hear it ring in the outer office.

Lessing came in almost immediately, carrying a homburg, a cane, and gloves. Potter's large blue eyes had an innocent, wondering expression. He half-rose from his chair.

"Take a seat, Mr. Lessing. What can I do for you?" There was no false bonhomie about him, and his voice was cold. A high starched collar with a cravat increased the impression of thinness, his neck looked scraggy and unhealthy. His complexion was bad, and he shaved only half way up his lean cheeks.

"Tell you the truth, I don't yet know," said Lessing amiably. He had a trick of giving the impression of trying to repress impatience. He had good features and a look of strength, without geniality. "There are one or two things you might be able to help with. We've got one thing in common, at least. We don't see eye to eye with the police and their conventional methods of investigating crime."

"In what way have you been crossing the police?" demanded Potter.

"They're crossing me. I'm not satisfied that they're right about the verdicts in the Prendergast deaths," Mark stated flatly.

Potter said acidly: "Mr. Lessing, if you have come to try to discuss anything concerning the Prendergasts you are wasting your time. I am acting on behalf of Mr. and Mrs. Claude Prendergast. They are fully satisfied with the verdicts returned, and with the attitude of the police. I am, too."

"Are you indeed?" said Mark. "Claude P. is in capable hands, that's something to know. Rather a pathetic little person, isn't he? Money, money everywhere, and no knowledge how to spend."

"I have no doubt that Mr. Prendergast would be grateful for your interest in him," said Potter. "I am equally sure that you have no reason for it. Mr. Lessing, I have often noticed how you apply yourself to other people's business. I must express the hope that in this instance you will break the habit. Your questioning of friends of Mr. Prendergast, and of his servants, has become most unwelcome. I am contemplating an application for an injunction to stop you from annoying my client. The idea is his own."

"Not Claude's. He doesn't have any ideas beyond the colour of his neck-ties and the cut of his trousers, plus the advantages of a piece of lemon or an onion or a Manhattan over a Martini. Maisie, though—"

Potter leaned forward.

"I shouldn't go any further, Mr Lessing. By calling here you have saved me the trouble of writing to you. I must ask you to stop this persecution forthwith. If you don't, I shall use every legal means to make you."

"Legal?" echoed Mark. "You've improved."

"Don't be impertinent!" Potter's eyes and his voice rose. "Get out of my office at once. If you don't I'll have you thrown out."

As he spoke, the door opened and a very large man appeared in the doorway. Large though he was, he was a difficult man to describe, being not exactly shapeless nor hulking, but vaguely like every other large man in the world. He had hair and eye-brows between-colours. His eyes were an indeterminate grey-blue. His voice was gruff as if he were suffering from a cold.

"Trouble, Guv'nor?"

"I may need you," Potter said sharply. "Wait outside."

Charlie Clay nodded, and backed out of the office. Potter turned his angry gaze towards Mark, who now sat on the corner of the big desk. His elbow was actually touching the envelope containing the photostat copies of his treatise.

"You know," said Mark, "life is full of coincidences. Last night my flat was burgled. Now I find Charlie Clay acting as your muscle man. I wonder if the police also know he's free, and know where he was last night."

Potter said: "I won't warn you again."

Mark smiled, and went out.

Near Clay another large man was standing. He was dressed in morning clothes and carrying a grey topper. The dress and the hat were incongruous, for the face of the wearer was rugged and chunky. He was Gabriel Potter's managing-clerk, according to the salary list, but in fact he had a variety of jobs, including that of bank messenger.

"Hallo, gents," said Mark. He ignored two scowls as he went out of the large general office. He dallied on the stairs, hearing approaching footsteps heavy and deliberate. There was a lift at Potter's office, but it was not working. In Mark's experience the lift never worked if anyone wanted to get to Potter's office in a hurry.

Then two more large men appeared, and one of them said: " 'Morning, Mr. Lessing."

"Nice work, Roger," Mark enthused. "They're after Clay."

Outside, he waited in brilliant sunshine by a tobacconist's in whose window was a large sign.

"No Cigs, No Tobacco, matches, flints–don't blame me, I can't help it."

The effects of war-time shortages were still acute.

Mark waited in the busy Strand for fifteen minutes, until a small crowd appeared at the entrance to the block of offices. The C.I.D. sergeant came first, Charlie Clay followed, Potter by his side, and the other plainclothes man brought up the rear.

"Potter's office is empty. Is this where I burn my fingers?" Mark knew that if he broke the law by going into Potter's office, Roger could not help him, but he never would have another chance like this. He moved across the road and entered the building again. He tried the lift, and found that it was now working. He went up to the fifth floor, half of which was Potter's, the other half being shared by three small firms. Two of the latter were empty, according to notices on the plate-glass doors.

No one was in sight.

Mark walked along the rubber-covered passage, past the door marked *"Potter & Son, Solicitors, Inquiries"* to one which announced: *"Potter & Son, Private."* He examined the lock.

"As I don't carry dynamite, that's no good," he said aloud. He lingered by the door, which was fitted with a brass Landon only an expert cracksman could force, and then only with the necessary tools and with plenty of time. Then he stood in the passage, hopefully. Before long, he heard the whine of the lift, and stood out of sight.

As the lift rose, he saw a tiny red hat, beneath it a thatch of reddish hair, beneath that in turn the big and heavily-rouged features of Maisie Prendergast. Reaching only just above the level of her shoulder was the top of her husband's fair head. Mark kept out of sight as the Prendergasts stepped past him, and went to Potter's office.

Maisie's fat, beringed hand was clutching her husband's arm. Claude was wearing pale pink corduroy trousers, a waisted sports jacket and a red shirt, the collar of which rode above his coat. Vast crepe rubber soles made him look splay-footed. Maisie's hat provided all her colour, except cosmetics and red shoes; her two-piece costume was of dead black. Across the shoulder and the hips she made two of Claude, and her dressmaker had under-estimated the size of her posterior.

The door closed on them.

Mark approached it, in time to hear Maisie declare loudly:

"But there must be some mistake." Her effort to refine her coarse voice would have been funny in other circumstances, but Mark was in no mood to see the funny side. "We had an appointment for twelve noon. Didn't we, Claude?"

"We did indeed," answered Claude.

"Mr. Potter *wouldn't* keep me waiting," went on Maisie, implying: *"mustn't."*

A girl was full of apologies. Mr. Potter had been called away unexpectedly, but there was no doubt that he would be back just as soon as possible. Would they wait? No, said Maisie, it was such an uncomfortable office to wait in, she couldn't understand why Mr. Potter did not pay more attention to the comfort and convenience of his clients. They would go across the road and have an early lunch at Mott's. Mr. Potter would find them there when he returned.

Mark went down by the stairs, and was out of sight when the

Prendergasts reached the lift. He was in the Strand in time to see them crossing the road and entering Mott's Chop House.

He weighed up the situation carefully.

By suggesting his visit to Potter, Roger West had admitted that he shared his, Mark's, suspicions. The fact that the police had found Clay in Potter's office meant that Potter was under suspicion. But there was a limit to what the police could do. Mark Lessing doubted if they could keep up surveillance of Potter's office for long.

"Yet Potter needs watching," Mark said aloud. He reached another building in the Strand, nearer Trafalgar Square; Potter's offices were between Aldwych and Fleet Street. This time a lift with a boy in attendance took him to another fifth floor, and he entered by a door marked: *"Morgan & Morgan, Private Inquiries."*

A small outer office was occupied by a typist at her machine, with a little fat man sitting on the corner of her desk. His red face and bulbous nose were familiar throughout London police courts, and particularly well-known in the Law Courts; it was related that Pep Morgan had given more evidence in divorce suits than any man alive.

He swung off the desk, his brightly polished shoes twinkling over the brown linoleum.

"Good morning, Mr. Lessing! Nice to see you again. Get that started, Flo, I'll finish it as soon as Mr. Lessing is through with me." He pumped Mark's hand and led the way to an inner office.

"Now what's troubling you?" he demanded, proffering a cigarette case. "Can't Inspector West help you this time?"

"The law is the law, and the Inspector a part of it," replied Mark. "If only he would retire! He and I together, Pep, would put you out of business in a fortnight."

"You'd be coming round begging for help before you'd been established a week," chuckled Morgan.

"Seriously, Pep," said Mark. "The Prendergast affair—"

"Still worrying about that? Let sleeping dogs lie, that's my advice."

"The trouble is *I* can't sleep. Can you put a man or two to keep an eye on Potter's office, and let me have a list of his visitors?"

"Gabby's a cool 'un, you know. Had this business for twenty-five years, and I wouldn't like to say how many times he's done enough for a seven years sentence. If he can snap his fingers at the police, he can snap them at anyone. I should hate to annoy Gabby."

"My flat was burgled last night, probably by a man named Clay who has just been arrested in Potter's office. He may have been reporting on his mission."

"Or he may have been asking for legal help. I'd rather the police did the watching."

"The police won't tell me what they find even if they watch. Just the names of his callers, that's all I ask, Pep. If you should happen to learn where he goes and who he goes to see, I wouldn't mind hearing that, too."

"I know what you want," Morgan said. "Everything and anything you can get about Gabby Potter. I'm not saying it couldn't be done, but I wouldn't like Gabby to know I had anything to do with it. I'm wondering whether you know how many people who offend Gabby get beaten-up? I wouldn't say that he knew anything about that," Morgan went on cautiously, "but it's a funny coincidence. I've known two or three people who thought they could find something about him, and after they'd tried they had a very nasty experience, and finished up in hospital. Handsome West knows it as well as I do. If he can't get Potter, what chance have I got?"

"Well, if you won't, Pep—"

"I'll tell you what," interrupted Morgan. "I know a man who might do it. He does odd jobs for me but isn't well known. Just leave it to me. I'll telephone you this afternoon if I can't fix it for you. Er—does Handsome know about it?"

"No," answered Mark, "but I'll make sure he learns how helpful you've been."

"If you ask me, Handsome will run into trouble one of these

days. The VIPs won't take kindly to having him cut through red tape. He's young, you know, and could do with a bit of experience, but if he keeps his nose clean, he'll go places."

"And if he becomes a Yard VIP you'll be glad you cooperated with his friend Lessing," Mark observed.

They both laughed.

4

FAMILY SUSPICION

Charlie Clay had two things in his favour, Roger soon learned; an alibi and a legal adviser. Potter stayed while Roger questioned him, and put in caustic comments from time to time.

Charlie, Roger inferred, had been told on the East End grapevine that the police were after him, and had rushed to Potter's office for legal aid.

"It's quite clear that there is no justification at all for this persecution of my client, Inspector. He can prove he was nowhere near this Mr. Lessing's flat last night. I think a letter or two to the newspapers might ensure that a man who is striving in every way to lead a straightforward and honest life will not be badgered by unimaginative policemen. You must realize the delicacy of your position, Inspector."

Roger said shortly: "Take him away, but if we break that alibi, look out."

"You cannot do the impossible," Potter said coldly.

He went out with a hand on Clay's arm.

Roger stared out of the window of the interviewing room, reflecting that Potter might try to cause trouble. He went off moodily to lunch. When he returned to the office he was buttonholed by an eager Eddie Day:

"You're for it, Handsome. The AC's after you. I think Potter got on the phone to him. Said he'd ring again. Mark my words, you'll slip up one day if you don't stop working out-of-hours with your friend Lessing. He put you on to Charlie Clay, didn't he?"

"Charlie Clay's fingerprints did," answered Roger.

Ten minutes later a curt voice requested his presence in the Assistant Commissioner's room. Curtness was not particularly alarming, for the voice was that of the AC's secretary, who had never been known to be anything but brusque. The AC was a man of moods, Roger knew, and particularly touchy about newspaper criticism, which Potter had threatened.

Sir Guy Chatworth was sitting behind his large highly polished desk in his highly polished office with electric light shining on his pale, highly polished cranium. He had a fringe of dark brown hair, flecked with grey, and a deceptive appearance of amiability. He looked like a prosperous country doctor, not a soldier turned policeman.

"Ah, West. I'm glad you're back. I want a word with you. Pull up a chair."

Chatworth at his friendliest was Chatworth at his most dangerous. His affability could become acid criticism. All he needed to do now to prepare a general assault on the follies of young inspectors was to offer cigarettes.

"Have a cigarette," he said, pushing a silver box over. "A light—" He flicked a lighter into flame and leaned forward, the flame reflecting on his polished head. "Now, West, I think you can give me some explanation of a peculiar state of affairs which has existed, I believe, for some time. Your interest, which appears to be more personal than professional, in the Prendergast family."

"I'm rather at a loss to understand you, sir," Roger said.

"Indeed?" Chatworth raised his eyebrows. "I had hoped that my approach was lucid, but of course I stand corrected." Sarcastic old devil. "Let me frame my question in a way which cannot be misunderstood. Are you satisfied with the inquest verdicts on the three Prendergasts?"

"No, sir."

"Have you ceased giving the matter your consideration?"

"No."

"Ah." Chatworth's voice lost its purr. "I'm glad you have been so frank. I am equally glad that you realize that the inquest verdicts were wrong. How much time are you spending on the case?"

Unbelievingly, Roger thought: "He's with me!"

"Officially, none, sir," he said. "I've given a lot of thought to it, at home, and——"

"With Mr. Lessing's help?"

Roger gulped. "We have discussed it, yes, sir."

"Interesting man, Mark Lessing," observed Chatworth. "If he were a pathologist, now—well, he isn't. But he has a good mind and an extensive knowledge of criminology. Rather given to intuitions, though. A dangerous proclivity. West, I have had a number of varied reports during the past few hours, and I gather that Lessing was visited last night and assaulted, and that afterwards his flat was ransacked. I gather also that you were on the spot in a remarkably short time, that no effort to catch the men was omitted, that you thought Clay was one of the pair, and that Mr. Gabriel Potter resented your interest in Clay. I infer—nothing in my reports suggest it, but I infer—that you think Lessing has deliberately proclaimed interest to goad someone to attack him, and you think he has succeeded."

"I do," Roger admitted, dry-mouthed. Was this benignity real?

"You might be right, too," Chatworth said bluffly. "I don't like to hear that Potter's taken over the legal side of the Prendergast business. I dislike Potter as much as you do, but I may respect him more. Still—there is a possibility that three murders have been done. I think I dare risk incurring some opprobrium by investigating the possibility. Be careful with Potter. Beware of him. But worry him."

Roger said: "Do I understand, sir, that I am detailed to investigate the Prendergast deaths?"

"Shall we say for two weeks?" suggested Chatworth. He pushed his chair back. He was big, burly, and impressive. "That's all, just now. Keep me advised, call for help as little as possible, and tell your friend Lessing from me that he must not take too many risks, nor disregard the general principles of the law, not even with Potter. Perhaps I should say especially not with Potter."

He nodded, smiled, and sat down, while Roger went out brushing his hand over his forehead; it was damp.

Half an hour later, when he let himself into his house he almost fell over the kitten.

"What, still here?" he asked. "Bless your padded feet, stay at least until this show's over."

He stopped, for Janet opened the lounge door. Beyond her, sitting in an easy chair with his profile showing, was Claude Prendergast.

· · · ·

Roger had dealt only with the third Prendergast death, which had taken place in London. As such, he had been obliged to look on Claude with the sympathy one would extend to a man suddenly bereaved of his whole family while enjoying something like half-a-million pounds as a consolation. Claude had shown no grief nor, Roger admitted, any great pleasure. He had remained a small-minded, vain, uneven-tempered little man who liked garish clothes, dancing, hot rhythm, alcohol in moderation, and a good time.

Janet put a finger to her lips.

"Hallo, darling, I didn't expect you so early." *Sotto voce:* "Mark brought him." She stood aside for him to enter, and instinctively he looked for Maisie; Maisie was not here. Mark was. He uncoiled himself from an easy chair as Claude's pink and white face grew more pink than white.

"Good evening," said Roger, smiling at Prendergast.

Prendergast rose, and extended a long, white hand, the best-formed part about him. His face was round and flat, his pale eyes were like limpid grey saucers, his fair hair was smarmed back and too heavily pomaded, and there were distinct bumps on his narrow head.

"Mr. Lessing suggested that—er—you might—er——" He looked at Janet.

"*Miaow*," called the kitten from outside.

"I'll go and look after that kitten," said Janet, tactfully.

Prendergast saw the door close behind her with obvious relief. Mark began to talk. He had been at his flat when Mr. Prendergast had called with a story which Roger should certainly hear— in an unofficial capacity, preferably. Mr. Prendergast fully understood that if any time came when it was impossible to treat it as a private matter then it would have to become a professional one. Not that there was anything for Scotland Yard, yet.

Claude lit a cigarette with a shaky hand.

"I'm dead scared, you mean," he said, and uttered a nervous little titter of a laugh. "Er—don't know that it's your pigeon, West. Only came here at Lessing's suggestion. Er—thought he was a private eye. You know what I mean." He tittered again. "Found out he isn't, or says he isn't. I—er—look here, Lessing, you'd better do the talking."

"Mr. Prendergast believes he has been followed about recently—he and his wife have been living at their London home —and twice he has nearly been run down by a car," Mark said flatly. "He suddenly realized that it is possible that his grandfather, father, and brother were murdered. He made another somewhat alarming discovery. He always believed that he was the last Prendergast. That isn't so. That is, he has a relative, a cousin, his father's sister's only son. He had heard vaguely that there had been an aunt, but nothing else. He gathered she had married without parental approval, and Claude thought it was a damned good thing, Grandfather Septimus having been a crotchety old man, Victorian to the last ditch. Wouldn't even permit cocktails, drank only port and Madeira."

Mark told the story with a manner so perfect an imitation of Claude's jerky delivery that it might have been a *verbatim* tape record. From time to time Claude nodded, and at the end broke in abruptly:

"You see what I mean, *Superintendent*," Roger smiled to himself at this piece of blarney, "Didn't think enough of the others to worry much whether they were dead or alive. Loosened the old purse-strings a bit, that was the main thing. Bit of a shock when Waverley, my brother, was bowled over. Often had a drink and a hundred up with him. Good sort, at heart. But I hadn't given a thought to murder. Should have realized what your questions were driving at, of course, but didn't. Knocked over, y'know. After all, half-a-million's half-a-million. There's the business, too. Only seen it as a source of free smokes before, but now—well, it's set me thinking. Couldn't let the business go to the dogs. As a matter of fact," went on Claude diffidently, "I had a bit of a tussle with my wife about that. She didn't see why I should suddenly become interested in *Dreem*, but a fellow can't help himself."

"Naturally not," Roger said.

"Then I learned about this unknown cousin," went on Claude. "Maisie, that's my wife, told me about him. Actually we had a bit of a row, and she asked me why the devil I didn't let someone with a business head run the business, if I was so keen on it. Then I wormed it out of her, there's this bloke Harrington."

Claude dried up, and leaned back in his chair. That Claude was a frightened man was more than obvious from his unsteady hands and quavering tenor voice.

Mark looked at Roger, and said:

"There's another thing, Roger. Mrs. Prendergast talks in her sleep, and—"

"I just can't understand it," Claude exclaimed, and uttered his ridiculous titter. "Never thought people did, if you know what I mean. Thought it was a figure of speech. But she did, this morning. I didn't catch all she said, but it was something about time I joined the others. I remembered what had happened *to* the others. Got under my skin. I was going to see my solicitor this morning, but he couldn't keep the appointment. Had some lunch, and Maisie said 'shall we join the others,' meaning some people at the next table who'd ordered claret. No taste for claret, myself, but—well, I realized what she'd said, then. My God, it's got me down! I knew Lessing had been asking a lot of questions and generally snooping, and Potter, that's my lawyer, said that Lessing fancied himself as a private detective. So I slipped round to see him. He persuaded me to come and see you."

"I'm very glad he did," said Roger. "I shouldn't worry, but people often talk in their sleep, you know."

"Dammit! I told you what my wife said."

"Your wife made a comment in her sleep which might have applied to anything. She may have been dreaming of a house-party, a dinner-party, a hundred-and-one things."

"That's what you think," retorted Claude. "I don't. Not now. I can't help feeling she hates my guts. Coarse way of putting it, but in the last few hours I've done some high-pressure thinking. She's *very* friendly with my solicitor. He was her solicitor first. We had a terrible quarrel just before I came away, and I think it safer to stay away for a bit. My God, I didn't think she'd got a mind like that!"

Roger sat without speaking. Mark looked out of the window. Prendergast brooded and peered into the fireplace.

He was at a high pitch of emotional excitement, Roger realized, being suddenly faced with a picture of violence and murder; he was seeing himself as a fourth victim, with his wife as one of the chief conspirators. In such a frame of mind, he should be easy to handle. A Prendergast who felt as frightened as he did was a godsend to the police and also a great danger to his wife and to Potter, *if* his fears were justified. So, Prendergast might be in two kinds of danger; from the murderer of his relations, and because he had cracked so badly.

"What shall I *do?*" he demanded.

Roger said easily: "Mark, can you spare some time in the next few days?"

"What for?" asked Mark, as if suspiciously.

"I thought as Mr. Prendergast has left home—temporarily, of course—he will want to stay in a hotel. If you could share a room, or a suite, with him, he would feel much safer. I don't think anything he has told us would justify police action, but I can understand why he is so edgy. Now if you—"

"Lessing!" cried Prendergast. "That's it. That's the answer. You must."

Both Roger and Prendergast looked at Lessing.

"I don't feel safe," Prendergast continued wildly, "I don't feel I dare walk up the street alone. Three relations killed, and—and now me."

"No one will kill you," said Roger. "You've done what none of the others had thought of doing—made sure of protection. If they were murdered, the deaths were made to seem accidental. No one can kill you accidentally while you've someone looking after you all the time. Will you do this, Mark?"

"You *must!*" cried Prendergast again. "I tell you—I beg you—"

"I'll make the time," Mark promised.

Claude Prendergast was almost maudlin in his thanks.

"We'll go down to Delaware," he said, "our country house, comfortable there. Better than a hotel. And since Maisie thinks I've left her she won't think of looking there."

"Can you tell me about your new-found relation?" Roger asked.

"Harrington? No. Only what my wife told me, and I've already told you that. Superintendent, I can't tell you how grateful I am. Really can't . . ."

When at last Mark and Prendergast had gone, Roger went into the kitchen. Janet was knitting, and the kitten playing with the wool.

"What made Claude behave like that?" Janet asked. "He was little better than a hysterical child. When he came in he kept looking over his shoulder, and implored Mark to stay by the window—even I heard that. Was that caused only by the quarrel with his wife? And this sudden fear?"

"I don't think so," said Roger slowly. "I think Claude broke down because he's been living on his nerves for a long time. No man, not even a Claude, would crack so completely on a flimsy piece of suspicion, if he were normal. I think that Claude might have been fed on drugs for some time. Whether he's been self-fed or not makes no odds. He's had the inheritance, the pitched battles with Maisie, and the drug. All of these have worked him up into his present state. I think he's broken out at the wrong moment for Potter and Maisie, too."

He stopped.

"Yes?" Janet leaned forward.

"The drug isn't a guess but a reasoned deduction. I wondered why Claude's eyes were so pin-pointed when I first saw them. I wonder what he's been taking? Cocaine would do it. Anyhow, Claude has been drugged, fact one. Maisie has talked of a long lost cousin, fact two. I had hoped to have the rest of the evening off, but I'd better get back to the Yard."

"I've seen that coming," Janet said. "Thank goodness I've a kitten to keep me company."

Petrol shortage and a conscience made Roger go to the Yard by bus, except in emergency. He walked to Fulham Road, caught a bus almost at once, and went to the top deck.

The new relation, Harrington, was on his mind; was there really one, he wondered? Or was this a scare from Maisie? Who *was* Maisie and where had she come from before she had married Claude? The sooner he could find out, the better.

Then he thought of the kitten, and grinned.

"Why are you so amused, Inspector?"

Roger turned sharply, to look into the face of Gabriel Potter. He checked his smile, and then widened it, edging closer to the window to allow Potter more room.

"And what brings you here?" he said.

"Finding you on the same bus—" Potter began.

"No," interrupted Roger. "Following or preceding me, but not finding. Were you coming to see me when you saw me at the bus stop? Or were you just around?"

"The meeting is entirely fortuitous," answered Potter. "If I wanted to see you, Inspector, I should call at your office, not at your private house. I had intended doing so tomorrow morning, but this may save my time. Inspector, I was annoyed, righteously annoyed, by your high-handed treatment of my client this morning."

"When did he become your client?" interrupted Roger. "Before last night's burglary and attack on Mr. Lessing, or after it? If before, why did he need a solicitor?"

"I think that you are a little drunk, Inspector," murmured Potter. "I have handled Mr. Clay's affairs for some years."

"Three times he took what wasn't his'n, three times he spent a spell in prison," said Roger amiably. "Either a hopeless case or a bad lawyer, and I wouldn't presume on the latter. Nothing about my "treatment" of Clay was high-handed. He is a specialist at a certain type of lock-cracking, and a lock was cracked in the specialist way he works, last night. He was known to be in London, too."

"I trust you are now satisfied that he was nowhere near Chelsea," Potter said coldly.

"Not for a minute." In Roger's mind's eye there was a picture of Chatworth's rubicund face, Chatworth giving him the go-ahead with Potter. He could have laughed in the solicitor's face. "I think Clay did that job, and his alibi was faked. You wouldn't know anything about that, of course."

"If I thought it for a moment, he would no longer be a client of mine," declared Potter.

"Don't apply the rule to your clients too generally," advised Roger. "You'll soon be on the bread-line."

Potter stared at him, and then deliberately stood up and moved to another seat. Roger continued to smile, but only for Potter's benefit; the phase of high spirits had gone.

Why should Potter take this extraordinary course? Had he really followed Claude, and hoped to find out what Claude wanted at Chelsea?

Roger stood up as the bus drew into Parliament Square. Potter remained on the top deck, staring out of the window.

"I'll be at the office fairly late," Roger said in passing. "Look me up if you feel like it."

He hurried down the stairs, nodded genially to the policeman on duty and went whistling towards his office. At a corner heavy footsteps materialized into the burly figure of Chatworth, dressed for out of doors. It was known that Chatworth disliked whistling, and talking above a whisper, in the passages. He glared at Roger, who bade him a polite goodnight.

" 'Night," growled Chatworth.

Roger made his way to his office and sat at his desk, glancing at one or two notes that had been put there since he had left. There was nothing concerning the Potter—Prendergast—Clay investigation.

He lifted the telephone, asked for Guildford Police Station and for Chief Inspector Lampard. He had met Lampard, who had conducted the inquiries into the first Prendergast death, near Delaware. A sound man, with no over-developed sense of his seniority, and who had said that he disliked the inquest verdict.

"Roger West here," began Roger. "You'll remember—"

"Remember." Lampard had a quick, decisive way of speaking, wasted no time in how-d'you-do's or reflections on the weather. "What do you want?"

"There's a job you might be able to help me with, Mr. Lampard. Claude Prendergast has just gone to Delaware House with a friend, a Mr. Mark Lessing. Lessing is acting unofficially for me."

"On what authority?" interrupted Lampard.

"No authority. He's in his private capacity only. Claude Prendergast has an idea that he might be number four on a list, and there could be something in it. Could Delaware House be watched?"

"Yes," said Lampard. "Anything to go on?"

"I'm no further than an 'if' and 'might be' stage, but I should hate to leave Claude unattended. Isn't there an AA phone box just near the house?"

"Yes."

"If anyone turns into the drive of the house," said Roger, "a word with Lessing might be advisable. I'm half expecting Mr. Potter or one of his clerks to go there, and possibly Mrs. Maisie Prendergast. Claude doesn't want to see her, he has peculiar ideas about her."

"So Potter's in this, is he?" Lampard grew expansive. "I'll do what I can, West. Anything else?"

"You'll be interested to hear that a new relative has appeared on the horizon," said Roger. "A man named Harrington. I'm trying to find him, but he hasn't made himself prominent yet. Does the name mean anything to you?"

"No," replied Lampard.

Roger renewed his thanks and rang off. He called *Information* and arranged for a teleprinter request for news of the man Harrington and for information about Claude's Maisie. That done, he cleared his desk, decided that he could go home, stepped to the door—and his telephone bell rang.

"A Mr. Gabriel Potter is in the hall, sir, asking to see you, a duty officer announced."

"I'll come down and see him," said Roger, and rang off.

He was beginning to feel very pleased with himself.

Potter was standing in the hall, homburg hat in hand, pointed chin riding high above his stiff collar. He carried an umbrella and pigskin gloves.

" 'Evening," said Roger brusquely. "Come along to the waiting room, it's warmer than my office." He led the way, and they settled themselves in two armchairs by the fire. Potter gave a thin-lipped smile.

"Your consideration is appreciated, Mr. West. If at any time I can reciprocate, I shall be only too glad." He made no reference to their meeting on the bus. "I wish to see you about Charlie Clay."

"Ah," said Roger.

"I have personally examined his story, and the witnesses of his presence last night in the Blue Dog, a public house in Wapping," said Potter. "There is no doubt that he was there during the evening, equally no doubt that he spent some time afterwards, until three o'clock this morning, in fact, in company of a woman." Potter's distaste grew into cold revulsion. "Earlier in the evening, he was the worse for liquor. Unsavoury, perhaps, but irrefutable."

"Why tell me about it?" Roger asked.

"I should dislike it intensely if you were ill-advised enough to take the matter further, only to find yourself blocked by evidence which the Court would have to accept! Unsuccessful prosecutions are not good for a young progressive officer."

"Thanks," said Roger dryly, and waited for the rest. Potter had not come solely about Clay's alibi.

"It occurred to me," went on Potter, "that you might have omitted to examine other possibilities in your eagerness to charge Clay. I did hear that a man named Fenton, Abie Fenton, was "out" last night. It might be wise to question Fenton. I hold no brief for the man," added Potter with a near approach to geniality, "and he is not my client. My object now, as always, is to see criminals pursued and prosecuted with the utmost vigour of the law." He stood up slowly, collected his hat and gloves, and showed his teeth. "Good night, Inspector."

"You've forgotten your umbrella," said Roger. He toyed with the idea of springing the name Harrington on the solicitor, but decided not to.

Potter went out with deliberate strides. Roger watched him thoughtfully, then tossed the stub of a cigarette into the fireplace.

Potter had thrown Abie Fenton at his head so heavily that he must know Roger would realize it was deliberate.

Roger went back to the office, and telephoned instructions for a call to be put out for Fenton. He replaced the receiver and frowned.

"That's what Potter wanted, of course, and he's got it. I wonder if that's what he was after all the time?"

He put on his hat and coat, and started for home. With luck he would get in just before Janet went to the next-door neighbours. There was little he could do that night, except to wonder what was happening at Delaware House and whether Mark had made Claude talk even more.

The front door opened as he turned into the gate.

"Darling," Janet called. "Mark just telephoned from Delaware House. He says that Cousin Harrington's there. Can you go at once?" Breathlessly, she added: "I told him *we* would go. We *can* go by road for this, can't we?" she wheedled.

"We can use the car," Roger agreed.

As he got the car out, feeling sure that Mark would not have summoned him without good reason, he wondered how far he would have got in this investigation without Mark. There was a lot to be said for an investigator not attached to the Yard, but there was the danger that Mark would be much more vulnerable than he.

Anxious and eager, knowing that Janet was happy to sit and watch the passing traffic in this rare luxury of a drive in days of petrol famine, he drove fast out of London towards the countryside, Guildford and Delaware House.

5

DARK NIGHT

"Do you think we'll make Delaware House before dark?" Janet asked.

"Not by half-an-hour," said Roger.

He was optimistic by twenty minutes, for on the approaches to Guildford it grew dark. He had to go slowly through the Surrey cathedral city, then turn by the bridge and find the road to Chesham, a small town not far from Guildford. Beyond it was Delaware Village, and Delaware House, the mansion on the pine-clad hills, which the Prendergasts had bought years ago out of the proceeds of *Dreem* cigarettes and tobacco. The road was in poor condition, one of those not selected for repair in war time, and every hundred yards ended in a corner. Faint objects flitted past them, telegraph poles, a cyclist without lights, a creature which swooped across the headlights.

"Ugh, a bat," said Janet.

"An owl, more likely. Creepy place, in the dark." He went on cautiously, knowing that he was looking for a turning to the left, anxious not to overshoot it. The overhanging branches of trees growing close to the road dragged noisily across the roof of the small car. The going grew steep, high banks on either side showed a ghostly yellow. The trees made shadows which seemed to move towards them and then sag away. Beyond were stretches of silent common-land, wooded in many places, he knew, with only an occasional farm or hamlet.

As he began to turn at a T-junction with a ghostly white sign, he saw the beams of another car coming from the side turning. He kept well in, realizing that the other car was coming at a suicidal speed for such a road.

Janet drew in a sharp breath.

Roger squeezed as close to the hedge as he could. As the car leapt at them, he was dazzled by the glare of the masked headlight. He uttered a silent prayer as his engine stalled.

The car scraped past them, brakes squealing, and swung right towards Guildford.

Roger re-started the engine.

"I'd like that driver in dock," he said. "I wonder where he came from? There can't be many places up here."

"Mark's pretty crazy at the wheel."

"Not that crazy," Roger replied, driving even more cautiously.

There were two entrances to Delaware, the one he was taking being inside the large estate which joined up with the major driveway near the A A box he had mentioned to Lampard.

Janet was peering out on her side.

"There's the gate," she announced.

The white gate was wide open, and Roger drove through. The road twisted and turned amongst shrubberies and copses, and the shadows increased.

Then Janet exclaimed: "Look! Look over there!"

Roger put on the brakes. Janet was peering to the right, and he followed her example. He saw nothing but the grotesque shapes of small trees and wild shrubs.

"I thought I saw a man," said Janet defensively. "In fact I'm sure I did, he—look! There's a cigarette glowing red!"

"I think we'll stop here," said Roger. He opened his door, while Janet scrambled out on the other side, joining him before he moved towards the main gate. The figure of the man remained clear in the headlights.

"I'm Chief Inspector West," Roger called. "Are you from Inspector Lampard?"

"That's right, sir." The big man's face was in the shadow; the light revealed him clearly only as high as his waist.

"Are there any others watching?"

"I'm the only one on duty at the moment, sir. Another man is coming to join me later. He would have been here but he had a puncture."

"Have you seen anything unusual?"

"No, sir. Had there been, I should have seen it. I can see both roads from here."

"So the mad driver didn't come from here," Roger remarked to Janet as they drove on.

The house soon loomed out of the darkness, but not until they had drawn up outside did they see its square shape against the starlit sky. A faint wind rustled about the tall trees growing near it. An owl gave a strident hoot which made Janet start. From the house there was no glimmer of light.

"The black-out's pretty good," said Roger. He left the rear and sidelights of the car on, and shone his torch on the steps. A bell clanged in the distance when he pulled the brass handle. After a short silence footsteps sounded.

A glow of light appeared, and Roger said:

"Mr. and Mrs. West, to see Mr. Prendergast."

"You are expected, sir," a man informed him. "Will you please come in. Can I fetch anything from your car, sir? Your case?"

"No, thanks." Roger held Janet's elbow as they stepped into the large, square hall. The rooms at Delaware House had one thing in common; all were square and all high-ceilinged.

Beyond the black-out trap the light was bright. The servant, an elderly man, led the way to a room on the right.

He tapped, opened the door, and announced "Mr. and Mrs. West."

Janet and Roger went through, to find Mark sitting in a comfortable chair, Claude Prendergast not so much at ease on a settee, and a tall, well-built man standing by the fire, which glowed red. There was no other light in the room until the servant switched it on. Then a dozen lamps in an ornate chandelier gave a garish yet dulled effect, a queer combination.

The tall man eyed them both curiously; while Roger had a shock. For Harrington, and this was Harrington, was not a day more than thirty. He had clear-cut features, was almost swarthy, had the look of a man in fine physical condition. He had clear, wide-set grey eyes.

Mark introduced everybody, and suggested drinks. He mixed gin and tonic, whisky and soda, and gin and Dubonnets. Claude appeared willing to surrender his position as host. He had made no more than a pretence at getting up, and now peered at Janet with lacklustre eyes; he looked very warm.

Harrington was eyeing her with the overt admiration of a man who expected to be a success with a woman.

"I'm glad you've arrived," he said briskly. His voice increased the good impression. "Now perhaps we'll get the official police view." His voice and smile were pleasant enough; but his manner suggested that he was irritated, though doing his best to conceal it. "Mr. Lessing has been very mysterious, and implied that you were the cause of police interest."

"Mark makes a mystery out of trifles," Roger said lightly. "I'm glad to have the chance of meeting you, Mr. Harrington."

Harrington accepted a cigarette. He was bigger than he had at first appeared; powerful, striking-looking. His dark hair was short and wiry.

"Why?" he asked.

Roger looked at Mark. "What *have* you been doing?"

"Looking around," said Mark, airily. "There's a cabinet full of old Dresden that's a delight, Roger, it rather took my mind off things."

Harrington said drily:

"Mr. Lessing has been entertaining me with a discourse on rare china. My cousin has hardly said a word. I hope you will be more informative."

Mark had obviously been stalling while Claude had been unable to hide his suspicions of his cousin. But *was* Harrington a cousin? He was a tough, hard man, very unlike Claude, unlike the other Prendergasts. An idea sneaked up on him: that Potter might have put Harrington up to pretend to be a relative.

Janet said abruptly: "Mark, did you know the house is surrounded by men?" She meant the police but Claude misunderstood. He moved quickly for the first time, jumping to his feet, and backing towards a wall. He held a hand in front of him, as if to fend off an attack.

"I knew it, I knew that would happen!" He swung round on Harrington, and his voice rose. "You brought them. You brought them!"

Harrington eyed him contemptuously.

"I'm going to get out of this madhouse while I'm still sane," he said. "I was never interested in the Prendergast side of the family. It was a mistake to try to get to know it." He moved very fast, and reached the door before Roger said:

"It's an unusual situation, Harrington, and I'm surprised you haven't been told about it. Mr. Prendergast is nervous because he expects an attack on his life. Mr. Lessing promised not to tell you, until I arrived. But don't let me detain you."

Harrington looked round.

"How much of that is bally-hoo?"

"No one here suggested that you should come. But if you want to know why your uncle is nervous, you should stay."

Harrington came back into the middle of the room. Roger gave a résumé of the half-suspicions and Claude's fears.

"Well, well," said Harrington, when it was done. "So he thinks I'm here to murder him for his money. In point of fact, Cousin Claude—" he sneered the name—"I am not interested in *Dreem* profits. I make plenty of money as it is. I came here because I'd grown curious. The family's been in the headlines a lot lately. I received a letter suggesting that I might be mentioned in one will or another, and that tickled my curiosity but not my greed. Prendergast money is dirty money by now, I should think. Didn't you know that?"

Roger ignored the comment.

"Who sent you the letter?"

"A solicitor named Gabriel Potter."

He must have seen that he had created something close to a sensation. Roger frowned. Mark said *"Well, well!"* Janet sat down heavily on the arm of the settee. Claude exclaimed after a short pause:

"*Potter* said you would be interested? *Potter?* That devil, he's behind this. That's why she took me to him!"

Something ought to be done about Claude. Roger wanted a rational talk with Harrington, but was not likely to get it with Claude present. He saw the grey pallor spread over Claude's cheeks, and believed that he was suffering from the strain that had affected him at Fulham. There was something unnatural about the man. There was a beading of sweat on his forehead, and on his upper lip.

"I can't stand any more of this," he muttered. He passed a hand across his brow. The perspiration there surprised him; he stared at his wet hand in bewilderment, and then drew a deep breath. He was shivering. "I just can't stand it. I feel ill. I don't think I'm well." He leaned back in the corner of the settee and closed his eyes.

Harrington glanced at Roger, puzzled, doubting.

Roger said softly: "He *is* ill."

Mark reached the little man's side.

"You'd better go to bed. I'll come up to your room with you." He eased the man up. Claude made no attempt to resist or to help himself, but staggered and grabbed a table for added support. His face was now a fiery red, and he kept licking his lips.

"Gi-give me a drink, will you?"

Roger was halfway towards the cabinet when Claude gave another exclamation. His knees bent and his legs doubled up. He fell so unexpectedly that Mark could only break his fall. He lay still, breathing stertorously.

"He's passed out," Mark said.

"He needs a doctor," declared Janet.

Harrington neither moved nor spoke.

6

CLAUDE AS WELL?

The old manservant was able to tell them the local doctor's name and telephone number. The name was Tenby. Roger knew of him as a police surgeon.

Claude was carried by Harrington and Mark to his room. The servants fussed and scurried, taken by surprise like the three visitors.

Roger went to the telephone.

Dr. Tenby promised to come at once when he heard that the call was from Delaware. Into his mind, Roger imagined, had sprung the same thought as to his, Mark's, Janet's and, judging from their demeanour, the servants'; that the last of the older Prendergasts was going the way of the others.

The servants were all old or middle-aged, and had been with the family for years. He wondered how much they could tell of the history of the family and whether it would be interesting. He would find out later. This was Lampard's district.

Roger telephoned the Guildford Police Station.

Lampard was not there, but Roger was given the Guildford Inspector's private number and called it.

Lampard answered, curtly.

Roger explained.

"I'll come over," Lampard said. "Thanks for ringing."

Janet came down with Harrington as Roger finished telephoning. The man was a head taller than Janet, and quite composed.

Mark was staying with Claude, Janet reported.

"I'm beginning to think my cousin is genuinely frightened, whether there's any need or not," said Harrington. "That collapse wasn't natural—there was something odd about it."

"Yes," said Roger dryly. "There are a lot of peculiar things in this affair. Three accidental deaths in a row. A solicitor who doesn't keep a client fully informed. A wife—Claude's—who told her husband that he would be wiser to leave the *Dreem* tobacco business to a business man, presumably you. Have you been approached to take any active part in the company's affairs?"

"No." Harrington was vehement. "I should have turned it down if I had been, anyhow. I'm not interested in *Dreem*. The company stinks." That was his second denunciatory reference to Prendergast, Blight & Company. Harrington lit a cigarette, flicked the match into the fire, and went on: "I came here because I was puzzled by several things. I had no idea that the Prendergasts even knew I existed, but they dug me out somehow. I had a letter from this woman Claude's married, and one from Potter. The implication of their conversation when I saw them was that I could expect to play a large part in Prendergast, Blight & Company."

"Did you talk as bluntly to them as to me?"

"No," Harrington admitted. "I stone-walled. It was no business of theirs, anyhow, but I was intrigued. Why should a solicitor and a woman just married into the family approach me, but not Claude? I decided to see Claude."

"Natural enough," said Roger. "Did you see Potter and Mrs. Prendergast together?"

"Yes. At the solicitor's office. The woman was like a tart with an expensive clientele."

"Who did the talking?"

51

"Mrs. Prendergast. Potter nodded a lot and looked like a cold fish. Is he always like that?"

"When he wants to be," Roger said. "Was anything in the way of a clear-cut proposition put to you?"

"No." Harrington threw the half-smoked cigarette into the fire. "That's what intrigued me most. They hinted at my taking an interest in *Dreem*, pointing out that Claude was the only member of the family left, and that he had no head for business as well as no desire to enter it. I had a feeling that some kind of bribe was in the offing, but they didn't get round to it."

"When was this meeting?"

"Yesterday morning."

"How did you know where to find Claude?"

"I'm working at Kingston," said Harrington. "I rang up the London house, thinking I could go there to see him. He wasn't there, but they gave me this address. It's not far from Kingston, so I decided to come on the off chance. I found Claude and your friend Lessing, who was very amiable but not informative, and they told me that you'd be able to explain more than they could. I was getting pretty tired of the mystery business before you arrived. It looked to me like another attempt to involve me."

It all sounded reasonable, and Harrington made it seem convincing.

The door opened and the old servant announced Dr. Tenby. Tenby was a short and stocky man, florid of face and abrupt in manner. He nodded to Roger and Harrington, bowed to Janet, and went upstairs. Soon afterwards, Mark came down.

As he came into the room, a scream broke the near silence. It went through Roger like a knife, and Janet jumped wildly.

It was high-pitched; obviously from a woman; and came from above their heads. Roger broke into a run for the door. Harrington beat Mark to it by a foot. Janet stayed by the fire, white-faced, fearful of a repetition.

There was none, but someone was crying near the landing.

Hurried footsteps thudded. Roger was halfway up the stairs when he saw one of the servants, her hands over her face.

"What is it?" he demanded. "What's the matter?"

She took her hands away, and stared at him, so pale that she looked bloodless.

"A man," she gasped. "The study—"

"Come on!" said Harrington.

He was ahead of Roger when they reached the landing, then turned and hesitated.

"Second door on the right," Mark called.

Claude's room was to the left. From it Dr. Tenby showed himself. He disappeared from sight again when he saw the others. The old servant hovered about the landing as Roger turned the handle of the study door.

He thrust it open, stood aside for a moment, then ducked and ran in. The others followed in a rush.

The study window was open wide and the light was on. They saw the top of a man's head above the window-sill, and a pair of hands clinging on to the sill. Harrington went forward with Roger at his heels, but before they could touch the hands the man had dropped from sight.

"Got a torch?" demanded Harrington.

Roger, peering out and down, saw the figure of the man darting towards the big lawn, just visible in the yellow light. Roger climbed out, lowered himself gradually as the intruder had done. It was second nature to notice that the study had been ransacked. He saw a torch in Mark's hand, and Harrington heading for the window. Roger hung from the windowsill only for a moment. He didn't know how far it was, but he dropped.

Soft soil took his weight, and flower stems crunched. His knees doubled, but with little or no jar. He turned at once. The light was bright enough to show the man disappearing into a shrubbery perhaps thirty feet away.

Roger plunged after him.

He heard the rustling in the shrubbery, the cracking of twigs, the swish of shrubs. He reached the bushes, while the noises were still audible, but then his own progress made listening difficult, and muffled other sounds. Near the drive a torch light was shining; Lampard's policeman?

There was a patch of uneven meadowland between him and the road. Harrington caught him up, lighting their way with the torch which he had obtained. It was difficult going. Hollows and mounds made them stumble from side to side. Their progress was fairly quiet now, and occasionally they could hear the man in front.

They heard him padding along the hard surface of the road, and Roger realized that he was heading for the gate through which he and Janet had driven. Breathing heavily, he and Harrington turned left as they reached the road. Suddenly their quarry came into view, for a faint glow of light showed ahead of him.

"Car," gasped Harrington.

The car was coming along the road. Its headlights picked out the white-painted gates, and the running figure of a small man. Roger felt acutely disappointed because it was not Charlie Clay; Charlie could do a lot of things, but not make himself as small as that.

There had been two men at Mark's place last night.

The car itself did not appear in view. Its engine was loud enough to deaden the sound of their footsteps as the fugitive reached the gates and ran across the road. The car engine revved and roared.

"My God!" cried Harrington. "Look out, look!"

The car came into sight. Its radiator struck the running man, and sent him flying, not sideways but downwards on to the road. There was a sickening, crunching sound. The car lurched, then went on. A scream, that echoed high and wide about them, drowned the whine of the engine as the car gathered speed.

It was out of sight when Harrington and Roger reached the hideous remnants of what had been a man.

Experiences of London in the blitz had hardened Roger; but the suddenness and the deliberate brutality of the crime sickened him. Harrington switched off the torch, and said in a shaky voice:

"I'd like to get my hands on that driver."

"Will you go back to the house and telephone the police?" Roger asked. "The local inspector is on the way, but you'll find someone at headquarters." He gave the number. "You all right?"

"If you're worrying about me, don't," Harrington said. "Your friend Lessing should be here in a moment."

The shock of the murder had made Roger forget Mark. Now he looked about him, but there was no sign of anyone. Roger borrowed Harrington's torch, and began to examine the area. The smashed body was in the middle of the road. Nothing could pass.

"I'll have to move him," Roger said. "Shine your torch, and then keep it pointing down the road to stop anyone who comes along."

"We'll hear them coming," Harrington said. "I'll help you."

Before they had started, the whine of a car came out of the quiet, and the twin orbs of sidelights and a single headlamp masked according to regulations came into sight, on the shortcut from Guildford.

It was Lampard, with a sergeant. They were shaken by the killing, and talked in low voices as the body was moved, on a car rug, to the side of the narrow road. Soon the sergeant drove along the road to fetch the policeman on duty. He came back with two. Lampard stationed one with a torch to divert traffic at the actual point of impact. No other cars arrived until a squad of men, summoned by telephone, came out from Guildford.

It grew cold. A wind which had been gentle at first soon stiffened. Flashlights lit up the hedges and trees as photographs were taken, a floodlight was run from a police car. Roger stamped his feet against the cold, and wished Mark would show up. Harrington returned to the house with Lampard's sergeant, with orders to have the study door locked until Lampard and the photographers arrived.

Roger began to suffer a kind of delayed shock. He had no doubt that the car driver had waited for the fugitive, and run him down in cold blood.

Lampard made little comment, beyond:

"We'll get the swine."

In the floodlight the body, covered with an old canvas sheet, looked dark and sinister. Lampard joined Roger.

"Did you get a good look at him?"

"I got a look."

"Didn't recognize him, did you?"

Roger said: "It wouldn't surprise me." He knelt down and pulled the sheet away from the small face, which was unmarked. A little hooked nose, tiny cauliflower ears, a weak chin; this was a burglar named Abie Fenton. In Roger's mind, Potter's voice seemed to be speaking insidiously. On the bus and at the Yard Potter had implicated Abie Fenton, not Clay.

Now Abie Fenton was beyond everyone's reach.

"Why, *I* know him," said Lampard, with a rare flush of excitement. "Half a minute. He's been on wanted posters—*Fenton*. That's right, Fenton. Isn't it?"

"Yes," Roger agreed.

He was thinking: the three Prendergasts, now Fenton, and God knows who next.

He thought with a stab of fear: where the hell is Mark?

7

MARK

The glow of a cigarette in the darkness caught Mark Lessing's attention. He was twenty yards or so behind Roger and Harrington, for his coat had caught on a hook, and he had been a long time getting through the window. The glow puzzled him, but as he passed it he realized what it was. He did not draw up at once, but ran on for a few yards, then stepped on to the grass verge. He made no sound as he retraced his steps, peering through the dark night until the red glow showed again. It was farther away from the road than when he had first seen it, moving slowly across the thicket. The noise of a car engine sounded, followed by the squealing of brakes, but he did not let himself be distracted.

He took advantage of the car noises to hurry forward. He needed to go faster than his quarry, who was walking diagonally away.

The glow curved an arc towards the ground, and remained there, fading slowly.

They were at the edge of the copse, and a field stretched beyond, with the man's figure discernible. Narrowing his eyes, Mark could see the head and the shoulders. They stopped moving and a faint sound told Mark the other was climbing over a stile.

Mark followed into an open field.

The other's footsteps made a padding sound on the soft and

springy turf. The wind swept across the field, piercing, unpleasant.

Mark was thirty yards or more behind his quarry, and the wind was blowing into his face; there was little chance that he would be heard, certainly none that the man would hear him.

A second stile was different from the first. High hedges rose on either side. Mark caught his coat on the right hand side, and the jerk almost threw him. The other was walking more quickly along the road, away from the gates and from Roger's party.

Mark stepped into the roadway.

He heard a rustle of movement, half-turned, and saw a shadowy figure close behind him. He struck out, but before he struck the other, felt a heavy blow on the back of his head. He threw his hands up to keep off a second blow, and plunged forward, not losing consciousness but with a furious pain in his head. The second blow came, jolting his forearm. He threw himself forward, fear almost at screaming point.

He was aware of voices. A man flung himself at him, seeking for his throat. He remembered vividly the moment when he had been attacked in bed, believed that this was the same man. The pressure increased remorselessly. Mark felt his lungs swelling, tried to breathe, gasped and struggled.

He felt blackness sweeping over him like a great wave.

His two assailants dragged him into the hedge, and a torch shone into his face.

Charlie Clay said: "It's the b . . . Lessing."

"He's going to get his before long."

"We wanted the other so-and-so." Clay swore under his breath, and stirred Mark with his foot. "What do we do with him?"

"Leave him," said the other man. "He didn't recognize us."

"What would the Guv'nor say?"

"Let's lift him."

Clay bent his back and the other helped to hoist Mark on to Clay's shoulders. Clay staggered under the weight but recovered and began to walk along the road. Despite the burden he moved more quickly than his companion. They walked for five minutes before reaching a narrow path leading off the road. On either side stretched gorse-clad land, and here and there the black outline of fir trees stood against the stars.

Beneath their feet the fine sand of the path gave way. They slipped and slithered. Clay's breathing grew laboured, but he stuck it until the path began to slope upwards. He put Mark down.

"Let 'im roll down into the ditch."

"Go easy," the other said urgently.

Clay laid Mark on the side of the path and deliberately kicked him into a ditch. He lay huddled in it, out of sight, and unlikely to be discovered even by day in this stretch of country, which was wild and desolate.

"Tie 'is 'ands and feet," Clay ordered.

That was done, and a handkerchief was forced roughly into Mark's mouth. Then the others went on, by the light of the stars. The path led to a wicket gate and a small cottage. They passed this, reached a wide drive, and approached a house with a long roof showing unevenly against the star-lit sky. They went to a side door, which the smaller man opened with a key.

"Let's have some light," said Charlie Clay.

They stood blinking at one another in bright light, then went in different directions. Charlie walked heavily along a red-tiled passage towards a low, oak-beamed hall, and up a flight of oak stairs which turned in the middle at a half-landing. He had to duck to avoid hitting his head against the beams, and his shoulders hunched when he reached the landing and went along the main one of two passages.

He tapped at an iron-studded door.

Potter's thin voice came: "Come in."

Potter was sitting in a high-backed chair, a finely carved monk's seat. He was behind a leather-topped desk. His dark clothes and high collar, and the gloom in the room, which was lighted only by the flames from a blazing log fire in a red-brick fireplace, put the clock back. Potter looked like a soul-less judiciary, an image of Bloody Jefferies. The firelight made one side of his face red, and set the other in shadow, just a pale blur.

Clay gulped, and did not look towards the fireplace. Sitting there in a more modern chair was a man whose face was entirely hidden in shadow, but whose eyes glinted red in the dancing fire.

"Yes, Clay?" said Potter.

"Never got him," Clay said, after a deep breath. "Got the Lessing b . . ."

"Modify your language," Potter said coldly. "Where is Lessing? You haven't brought him here?"

"Took 'im off the road, and he's lying down by the 'ill. You know the place, just this side of the road. No one will find him this side of tomorrow's breakfast."

The man by the fire moved slightly.

"You witless fool," Potter said dispassionately. "Why didn't you leave him on the doorstep, and telephone for the police? Get him away from there at once. Take him to the other side of Delaware. Use one of the cars, and go the long way round. Is he badly hurt?"

"He won't forget the bonk on the head for a long time."

The man from the fireside spoke, clearing his throat and then saying:

"Why don't you bring him in and question him?"

"You are as big a fool as Clay," said Potter. "Lessing won't talk, whether he knows anything or not. After the discovery last night there's little chance that he has any idea of what is happening, beyond the broad outlines, and that won't help him at all. If we bring him here—"

"He needn't get away," the other said coldly.

"And we'd have an unnecessary corpse on our hands. Get one thought out of your head, Duke. We have been sailing far too close to the wind already." Despite the colloquialisms, his voice made the words sound pedantic. "All right, Clay. Report as soon as you are back."

Clay nodded, and went out.

Potter turned to a file of papers open on his desk, but made only a pretence at reading them; the light was not good enough to enable him to see more than the vague lines of writing. After a pause the man by the fireside said:

"How cold-blooded can you get?" He tried to get out of his chair, unsuccessfully. He glared at Potter, who returned his gaze evenly, then pushed the papers on one side and leaned back. He put his hands and forearms along the wooden arms; he needed only a flowing gown and skull cap to make him look like an Inquisitor from the dark ages, but the red firelight dancing on his face gave him a satyrish air.

"Duke, you sometimes forget that you, Clay, and the others are living on licence—*my* licence. Do you ever think of where you would be but for me?"

"You can cut that out," Duke retorted. "You're in as deep as any of us. You're through if we're through. Don't forget it. I'm tired of sitting around and doing what you say, I've been doing it for too long. When are you going to kill Harrington? The way you talked, you should have had him a month ago."

"He won't last much longer." Potter's thin hands bunched. "You don't seem to appreciate the difficulties. We nearly got through without a serious hitch, but the appearance of one more Prendergast was a serious obstacle. Three accidents—" his lips curled. "Three accidents were too many, and West was not alone in being suspicious. We might have got clear but for Lessing."

"He got you on the run," Duke declared. "You were crazy to go to his flat."

Potter said sharply: "He might have had those papers."

"Might have," sneered Duke. "Potter, I've been doing some thinking, and I don't like the way my mind's gone round. I'm asking myself if those papers ever disappeared. If I thought you'd pulled a fast one, I'd break your neck. You don't frighten me any more, and you never will. Were those papers ever stolen?"

Potter breathed hard through his nostrils.

"Yes, they were stolen. If the police find them, or if Lessing should, they'll finish you, Clay, and me. The police aren't going to find them, though."

"If Lessing didn't take them, who did?"

"I shall find out," said Potter.

"Haven't you any real idea?"

"At the moment, no."

"So someone's running around with a load of dynamite big enough to blow us all sky-high," Duke said. "Potter, you must have some idea who took them. Who would raid your house? Who could take that chance? You're working with others. *Who?* That's what I want to know."

"Be quiet!" snapped Potter. "I am working with others, yes. They are in high positions, and are far too reputable to have burgled the house or to have employed anyone to do it. I am working for men who will not take personal risks. They work through me. The prize was big and I took the chance. A great deal has gone wrong, but we can put it right if we keep our heads." He paused for a moment, and then said abruptly: "We will have a rehearsal. What is your name?"

Duke leaned back in his chair.

"Harrington. William Ellsworth Harrington."

"When were you born?"

"January 30, 1908."

"Where were you born?"

"19 Hemsley Road, Harrogate, Yorkshire."

"What was your mother's maiden name?"

"Prendergast, Emily Joanna. And I can do the rest without being prompted," Duke went on. "My father was William Ellsworth Harrington the first. He was a gentleman-farmer, too much gentleman and too little farmer. He died in 1914, in

France. My mother died in 1918, from the Asian influenza. I was brought up by an adopted aunt who made plenty of profit, my mother having left her all she'd got—a couple of thousand pounds or so. I escaped from auntie's loving care in August 1924, after leaving Harrogate Grammar School where I'd gone with a scholarship from Towngate Road School. I emigrated to South Africa, got tired of oranges and lemons and skipped it to Singapore, where I got tired of selling phoney jewellery to tourists. I had a dab at rubber-planting in Borneo and later in South Malaya. I got ideas about rubber and developed them, but was swindled out of my patents. I took a freighter to San Francisco, where I had some new ideas, and made a pile. I came back to England because of the war and joined the Navy."

"Why did you join the Navy?"

"I guess I liked salt water. I gave my name as Duke Conroy because I didn't want to let my family get in touch with me, and also because when I jumped Johore State my employers didn't like it and set the police after me. I thought I was wise to be *incognito*. I was torpedoed in the South Atlantic and badly smashed up. I still can't walk properly and I'm hoping English surgeons will be able to improve on the first sawbones. That's the story," Duke finished, "but I'm telling you that—"

"I will not have you—"

"You sit back and listen," Duke interrupted roughly. "I'm dumb but not so dumb. Maybe we could have put that line over if Harrington had been bumped off before Lessing and West learned about him, but since Claude Prendergast has gabbed, it's all through. I'm not going on with it."

"You will go on with it," Potter said, "or the police will learn that before you became 'Harrington' in South Africa you committed two murders in Southern Rhodesia. But we need not discuss that. Lessing and West know someone who calls himself Harrington, and part of his story. What of it? When Harrington's dead, there will be plenty of evidence that he is not the real son of Emily Joanna Harrington, wife of the late William Ellsworth, daughter of the late Septimus Prendergast. Harrington's identity will be discredited, and yours established."

"I tell you it won't work. West won't believe it."

"West will have to consider the evidence," said Potter. "I have the necessary documents proving that you are the genuine Harrington, and others proving that the Harrington now at Delaware is a fraud. Leave the legal side of this to me."

"Like hell I will. What's Harrington going to be—dumb all the time? Won't he spill his yarn to Lessing tonight? Even if he doesn't, what will the police do if he's killed?"

"When we get to Harrington he is not going to be killed, he is going to commit suicide. He will leave the necessary evidence that, with Abie Fenton and others, he arranged the murders of the Prendergasts. The evidence will be irrefutable, I shall see to that. The police will have their murder theory vindicated, and a dead murderer with a motive which stands up. Meanwhile, I shall have found you."

Duke drew a deep breath.

"Your spiel's good," he admitted slowly. "You make it sound as if it can work."

"Of course it can work. If the police try to prove Harrington's identity now, any papers they may find at his flat will be faked. I've made sure of that. Harrington will look like a phoney from the beginning—it will be an advantage rather than a disadvantage that the police have found him before we arrange his suicide. The police will dig more deeply, and find that you are the real Harrington, not Conroy, guilty of those two murders in Rhodesia, and—" Potter stopped, and showed his teeth. "Supporting evidence is always valuable, Duke. I hope that in future you will not be foolish enough to doubt whether I can or cannot make the necessary arrangements. Our concern is not Harrington, but the stolen documents. I shall know who has them by tomorrow."

"Or do you just mean you hope you will!"

"We will call the two words synonymous."

They stopped talking, Potter switched on a small table lamp and began reading through the papers on the desk. Duke picked up a magazine, and turned the pages idly. After half-an-hour he looked up and said:

"Clay's a long time."

"He is being thorough," Potter said, and went on reading.

But Clay did not arrive in the next hour.

8

NOT NICE FOR MARK

Roger was with Lampard and Dr. Tenby for over an hour after returning to Delaware. The telephone wires to London and to Guildford were kept busy. A nurse arrived from Guildford, and Dr. Tenby spent a lot of time with her in Claude's room. Claude was not dead, but his condition was serious. Tenby would commit himself no further than that he was suffering from a form of hypnotic poisoning and that he might be able to pull through. Meanwhile, his wife should be summoned.

Maisie was not at the Braddon Square house. The servants there gave a list of places where she might be, but did not seem optimistic about her being found.

Policemen from Guildford were reinforced by members of the local Home Guard platoon in a search for Mark Lessing; after an hour Janet refused to believe that Mark had disappeared voluntarily.

"He won't like the hunt for him if he's gone off on his own," Roger said.

"Never mind about that," Janet retorted. They were with Harrington in the lounge. "If he's gone away on some wild goose chase without letting us know, it's his fault if he's caused a sensation."

Harrington looked from her to Roger.

"Between you and me, I'm finding that a bit beyond me. Do things often happen this way?"

"About once in a thousand times. Don't imagine this is typical of a policeman's life. Normality is boring in every phase, ours not excepted. Whatever you call this, it isn't boring." Roger lit a cigarette and asked: "Can't you remember anything that Maisie Prendergast or Potter said which might give an idea why they contacted you?"

"They were vague all the way," Harrington said. "The only time they asked more than indirect questions was when they wanted to know what I'd been doing since I left England. I left when I was a boy," he added off-handedly. "My parents died early, and I learned that my mother had had the thick end of the stick from her family. In spite of all the *Dreem* millions, she died of influenza through lack of expert attention. It was only by an accident after she was dead that it was found she had a couple of thousand pounds' worth of *Dreem* shares. They went in trust to an aunt who brought me up—and she spent it all." Harrington's grey eyes grew thoughtful. "I've travelled a lot since then, but I've never forgotten those days."

"You've been on your own a great deal?"

"That hasn't anything to do with the past," said Harrington. He thrust his hands into his pockets and stared into the fire. "Is there any point in my staying any longer?"

"It's up to you," said Roger. "I'd be glad if you stayed, but I can't make you."

Harrington thrust his hands deeper in his pockets.

Then a sergeant called for a word with Lampard.

Harrington said:

"I'll be back in a few minutes."

The door closed on him. Roger put a hand at Janet's waist, and said lightly:

"Have I got competition?"

"I like Harrington," Janet declared. "He's sore, and he's got an awful load on his mind. Perhaps he's irritable after coming here and seeing what it would be like to be rich. What do you think of him?"

"Tough, resourceful, secretive, and possibly with a chip on his shoulder. Apart from the inheritance—and don't take any notice when he says he doesn't want *Dreem's* fortune—if he's brooded over a raw deal from the family, he could have killed for that. No, it's not likely, but it's on the cards. The more I think about the case," Roger went on slowly, "the worse it gets. That Fenton killing was absolutely cold-blooded, and we've at least one murder to solve. It increases the possibility that the Prendergasts were murdered, too. And Potter—damn it, Potter wouldn't be so obvious as to bring Fenton here and then plan the murder, so that I had a nice little witness, stone dead and uninformative."

"I don't like you when you talk like that," said Janet. "It makes you sound as callous as Lampard. Roger, do you think Claude was poisoned?"

"Of course he was," Roger said.

"I don't mean that," said Janet, "what I mean is—well, was he poisoned before he went to see Mark, *because* he was going to see Mark? Or would he have been killed in any case?"

"Good question," Roger said.

"I wish Mark would come," Janet said, restlessly, and then raised one hand. "My goodness, I'd forgotten! You know that little man Morgan—"

"Pep Morgan?"

"Yes. Isn't he a private detective?"

"There are other names for him."

"He called this evening, and left some notes for Mark," Janet said. "They're in my bag. He said that Mark was expecting them." She picked her bag up, and drew out an envelope. "Do you think we ought to open this?"

"No," said Roger. He took the envelope, and ripped it open. As he read he raised one eyebrow. "It's a list of the people who have been in and out of Gabriel Potter's office, and of Gabriel's movements. Three people Pep couldn't identify called, as well as our Maisie, Sir Andrew McFallen and a Gregory Hauteby. Nothing startling. It's a pity."

"What's a pity?"

"That Mark's not at the Yard. He's got the right attitude towards routine investigating. Like you, I wish—"

The door opened, and Lampard put his head round it.

"We've found your pal Lessing," he announced, and withdrew without another word.

"Is he hurt?" cried Janet.

Roger hurried after Lampard, seeing Harrington come out of a cloakroom, rubbing the backs of his hands. The door leading to the domestic quarters was blocked open, and there were movements in the passage beyond—of men, and a stretcher.

"Oh, no!" exclaimed Janet. Her hand was tight on Roger's arm.

Mark was on the stretcher, and his face was colourless. There were scratches on his cheeks, an ugly bruise on the side of his face. But even from where they were standing they could see that he was breathing.

Lampard appeared by Roger's side.

"Found him in a ditch," he said briefly. "He doesn't seem too bad. Shall we take over a room here?" It was the first time Lampard had shown any indecision.

"With Claude *hors de combat*, Harrington's the host," said Roger. "Unless Maisie appears and we could tell her that Claude gave the permission." He turned to Harrington.

"It's all right with me, if that means anything."

The manservant, Petrie, was near the stretcher, with two elderly women. They hurried upstairs to prepare a room. Janet and the nurse from Claude's room spent ten minutes with Mark, and passed the same verdict as Lampard.

"I'll sit with him," Janet volunteered.

"I'll wait here until he's had a chance to come round," Lampard said. "Shall we take another look at the study?"

They went into the room from which Abie Fenton had run to his death. It was still in an untidy state, for although the police had searched the room, and photographs were already on the way to Guilford for developing, no one at the house might be expected to know where the papers littering the floor and desk had come from. It was a job for Claude or Maisie or one of the Prendergast employees.

"We'd better pile the stuff together on the desk," Roger said.

"Yes." But Lampard showed no inclination to begin. "Prints were all over the room," he went on. "I wonder if Fenton's are among them? What was Fenton's reputation?"

Roger was prompt. "A nice little man, for a burglar. He usually worked under orders, he wasn't an original mind. He didn't deserve what he got. By morning we'll have something from the Yard about his recent contacts." He offered cigarettes, but Lampard refused. "I haven't told you yet," he went on, "but I've been given a fortnight in which to concentrate on the Prendergast business. We're not alone in thinking the deaths murders."

Lampard made a remark about coroners under his breath.

"There isn't a lot of doubt now, surely. I'm glad you're handling it, Inspector. Now about Mr. Lessing." He was cold and brisk. "He was found on the side of a road about three miles due west of Delaware, although he started off in an easterly direction. It wasn't too far for him to walk in the time, but there's no reason for thinking he would walk in the direction he did." Lampard went on with the precision and facial expression of a machine-gun. "In his hair and on his clothes is a silvery sand found about here and towards the north-east, but not in the west. The soil changes, getting chalky where he was found. The blow on the head broke the skin, and some of the sand was in the wound."

"Nice work," Roger said. "So he wasn't attacked where he was found?"

"And he wasn't in a condition to walk from any district where the sand is found, to the spot we discovered him," Lampard went on. "He was taken by a car."

"Our man seems to run a fleet of them," Roger commented.

Lampard tightened his lips. "What is your view of tonight's events so far?"

Roger leaned against a chair.

"Too many ifs and too many mights, and if I had to put events in order of importance I'd say that the burglary is Number 1. Abie worked under direction. Presumably he knew the car which ran him down was waiting, that was why he made a bee-line for it instead of cutting through the undergrowth, where he had much more chance of dodging us. You know what I mean, there's a copse—"

"I know," said Lampard.

"If Abie thought an escape car was waiting for him, his employer bumped him off without having a chance of learning whether he had found anything in the study."

"Ah," said Lampard, and his lips curved a little.

"The employer would hardly have been ready to kill so quickly if he'd had any serious expectancy of getting anything useful from the study. Fenton had nothing from the house in his pockets, had he?"

"No, nothing at all. I'm glad you've reasoned that way, Inspector. I had, too, but wondered if I was cock-eyed." He actually smiled, his eyes gleaming for the first time since Roger had known him; Roger's earlier resentment of his brusque manner faded. "Two peculiar situations, then. One, that Mr. Lessing was removed from one part of the district to another. The second that Fenton was killed by someone who had sent him to burgle Delaware but was not interested in what he found."

Roger said slowly:

"Taking the second one first, Fenton's employer either sent him on the burglary simply because he wanted this chance of killing him, which doesn't seem likely, or he sent him to Delaware knowing that nothing was going to be found of interest, but wanting it known that he had been here."

"We're agreeing almost too much," Lampard said dryly.

"Something happened to make it necessary to kill Fenton," Roger said. "The obvious inference is that I was seen to arrive, and the employer was afraid that I might get a line on him through Fenton. Reasonable?"

"It is to me."

"So now back to the first peculiar situation," Roger said, with satisfaction. "Someone was very anxious to make sure that Mark wasn't known to have gone in the direction of the silver sand vicinity. Good idea, no doubt, but bad execution. Is there silver sand in a wide area?"

"Wide, but not thickly populated," said Lampard. "I'll have it searched by tomorrow midday. Why was Lessing here?" he added offhandedly.

Roger chuckled. "And why am I here? Because . . ."

He spent fifteen minutes giving Lampard a resumé of the situation. A sergeant looked in for the Guilford Inspector, with the report that Mr. Lessing was still unconscious, and the nurse thought the coalition might last for several hours.

Lampard nodded dismissal, and then said to Roger:

"Well, you've got your hands full. I'll get along—but count on me to do all I can. I'll keep in touch. Close touch. You'll let me know if anything big develops, won't you?"

"I certainly will," promised Roger.

He waited until he had heard the front door close on the Guilford man, then took Morgan's notes from his pocket, and read them again.

"Dear Mr. Lessing,

Glad to report that I've got that little job started. Three unknowns called on our friend P. this afternoon, as well as:

Mrs. Prendergast.
Sir Andrew McFallen.
Mr. Gregory Hauteby.

P. left around five o'clock, and my man lost him at Kingston. More tomorrow. Don't forget to mind your step.

     P.E.P.M."

Roger was still reading it when the door opened and Janet came in.

"How are the invalids?" Roger asked.

She didn't answer at once, and he studied her. His heart missed a beat, for she looked so lovely in her anxiety, with a kind of troubled calm. She had just combed her glossy, wavy dark hair, and dabbed powder on her face.

"Mark's all right—Dr. Tenby gave him a sedative to make sure he has some rest. I've peeped in to see Claude Prendergast. He looks terrible, but the nurse says he's no worse and is not in danger. To look at him you'd think he was at death's door." She saw the letter. "Does that help at all?"

"Read it." He watched as she did so, and saw her frown.

"Kingston's in this direction from London, isn't it?"

"Yes, Potter undoubtedly headed in this direction. However, that isn't the only thing. You wouldn't know, would you?"

"Know what?"

"About Sir Andrew McFallen and Gregory Hauteby," murmured Roger. "They are directors of *Dreem*, and now perhaps clients of Potter. Now tell me, why should two of the directors start contacting Potter, when as far as we know, they've never done business with him before?"

"You don't know everything," Janet murmured.

"A minute ago, I wanted to kiss you. No, I don't know everything, but I haven't brooded over this affair for several months and kept my mind closed all the time. Until now, McFallen and Hauteby have had no outward connection with Potter. We can check, of course, it won't take long. That leaves Widdison and Transom."

73

"If you go on being obscure, I'll find someone else to kiss me."

"Such as Harrington?"

"Dark romantic soul," said Janet. "I can imagine him being a real lady-killer. Who are Widdison and Transom?"

"The remaining directors of Prendergast, Blight & Company, more usually known as *Dreem*."

"You've had an idea," Janet said.

"I've been telling myself that the co-directors of *Dreem* could not reasonably be interested in the deaths of the Prendergast family, because once all four were *non est*—I mean dead—"

"I know my Latin," said Janet coldly.

"Once the Prendergasts were no longer able to take their position on the board of the company," continued Roger, with dignity, "their shares, which cover a majority, had to be put on the open market. Old Sep's will was most explicit. Shares on the open market, the *really* open market, can be snapped up by anyone. There would be stern competition for *Dreem* shares, which not only pay a dividend of 20% or so, but also would be in great demand by the other tobacco companies, who resent the independence of *Dreem*. Now Potter makes a big difference. He is not a stockbroker, but he may have clients who are, and other clients who would like to buy *Dreem* shares."

"I *think* I follow you," said Janet. "You want to find out if Potter's buying *Dreem* for someone else."

"Yes. If a combine—call it the A 1 Tobacco Company— bought up the Prendergasts' shares, Messers Hauteby, McFallen, Widdison, and Transom would be left out on a limb. They couldn't resist a take-over bid from A 1, and their strength wouldn't be enough to fight for good terms. I'll have to find out why they visited Potter, and what business they've been doing with him. I suppose there's been no internal trouble inside *Dreem*?"

"I wouldn't know," said Janet. After a pause, she stirred a ledger with the toe of her shoe. "This room's a helluva mess, darling. Shouldn't we do something about it? We might find something worth seeing, too." She kept stirring the ledger but looked wide-eyed at Roger, her most innocent expression. "Potter couldn't be trying to buy all the *Dreem* shares, could he? From 1, 2, 3, and 4, as well as the Prendergasts? After all, up to a point he has control of the Prendergast shares now, hasn't he? Through Claude, or Maisie. Or he thought he had, until Claude got obstroperous."

"Obstreperous," corrected Roger absently. "Come and be kissed, that *is* an idea."

A noise came from downstairs, some disturbance followed by a high-pitched voice alternating with Harrington's deeper one. The latter was so low in fact that it must be taken for granted that Harrington was talking. A door slammed, and the voices were cut off. Roger and Janet moved together towards the door.

It opened before they reached it, and old Petrie entered.

"Excuse me, sir," Petrie said. "I thought you should know that Mrs. Prendergast is downstairs."

"Thank you, you're quite right," said Roger. He went past the servant at once.

He knew that Maisie might have come because the news had reached her, but it seemed unlikely that she could have got to Delaware so quickly. He hurried down the stairs with Janet on his heels, and opened the door of the lounge. Maisie's strident voice was raised.

'Bloody impostor!" Maisie shrieked. "You lying skunk, you're no more William Ellsworth 'Arrington than I am! I'll have the law on you, I'll see you get what you've asked for. Get out, get out of my 'ouse."

9

MAISIE GOES WILD

Harrington was standing with both hands in his pockets, his back to the fire. He was staring at Maisie, who had thrown open an opulent grey mink coat, and was shaking one fist at him from a distance of about five feet. A small hat with a veil which dangled to her nose was too far forward on her head, and her thick legs were set apart.

Harrington said contemptuously:

"You're drunk."

"Drunk, am I?" squealed Maisie. She took a step forward. Roger studied her flushed face, her parted lips, and did not imagine the whisky fumes. Her clenched hand was trembling, but she remained at a safe distance from Harrington. Her poise suggested that she was prepared to jump out of danger. "You insulting tyke, get out of my 'ouse! Insult a lady, would you, call *me* drunk? What have you done to my 'usband? Where is he? That's what I want to know—*where's my 'usband?* Drunk?" She screeched the word at the top of her voice. "I'll give you drunk, you—you fake. You murdering double-crossing fake."

Roger stood by the open door, with Janet peering over his shoulder on tip-toe, and Petrie only a foot behind her.

Harrington did not appear to notice them; Maisie certainly did not as she drew a fresh breath.

"I'll have the law on you, I'll see you get 'ung for your murdering—murdering—murders! I'll see you strung up before I've finished. I know what you've done—*and where's my 'usband?* If you've done anything to him—"

Harrington looked across to the open door. Maisie ignored the gesture and burst into another wild diatribe. Roger went forward, and Janet made herself close the door on the outside. Petrie looked frail and troubled. Without a word, he went towards the domestic quarters. Janet opened the door an inch; there were limits to her self-restraint.

Roger was interrupting Maisie Prendergast's frenzied outpourings.

"Good evening, Mrs. Prendergast. I am Chief Inspector West . . ."

Maisie's voice was cut off as if by a knife, and she turned abruptly. Her foot caught against a mat, and she stumbled. Her hat fell further over her forehead, and she brushed it back with a jerky gesture. Roger was puzzled. Maisie had big, unexpectedly fine eyes, and they were neither bleary nor bloodshot. The rest of her was roaring drunk, but her eyes were stone cold sober.

"You!" she sneered, "you call yourself a policeman, and you let this swine stay in the same 'ouse! Clear him out, I won't have him here! Calls himself my Claude's cousin—cousin, baloney, if I'm not careful he'll do him in like he did the rest." Her aspirates were wildly uncertain, over-emphasized. She flung a quivering hand towards Harrington, but continued to glare at Roger.

"She's quite drunk," Harrington said coldly.

"Why, you—"

"We'd better quieten down," Roger said. "You'll disturb the invalids, Mrs. Prendergast. Your husband has been taken ill."

Her ugly mouth widened.

"I knew it, I knew it! Claude, where's my Claude? I'm going to see him. Stand out of my way, copper." She advanced a couple of paces, but stopped when Roger stood fast.

"Dr. Tenby has refused permission for anyone to see him," he said. "The doctor will be here again soon and you can ask him for permission then. Meanwhile, you have just made a serious accusation against Mr. Harrington." He was as cold and precise as Lampard.

"I'll accuse him all right!"

"Are you formally making a charge of murder against him?" Roger demanded. He saw a cunning glint in the big eyes. He was uncomfortably aware that Maisie was more clever than he had realized, that she might have outwitted him before because he had assumed she was a fool.

"That's a job for *you*," she breathed. She turned uncertainly, dropping heavily onto the settee. The springs groaned. "Oh, my poor, poor Claude. You, you dumb copper, didn't you realize there was something fishy about the way they all died? Didn't you never ask yourself no questions?" She took her handkerchief from a bag on her lap. The long handle of the bag was fastened to her fat, plump wrist. "Poor, poor Claude, the last of them. He's the last."

"Why did you say that this is not Mr. Harrington?"

"I—I don't know what I said!" evaded Maisie. "I can't stand the worry any longer, I just can't. It's too much for one person to bear."

She burst into tears.

Roger regarded her dispassionately. Harrington took a pipe from his pocket and began to fill it. Then Maisie startled them by jumping to her feet and rushing towards the door.

Outside, Janet moved away quickly.

Roger followed, and watched Maisie walking laboriously up the stairs, grasping the hand-rail to steady herself. She put her feet down heavily on each stair. Roger waited until she was nearly at the top, then followed. She made no attempt to go into Claude's room, but went into a bedroom next to it.

She appeared not to see Lampard's plainclothes man on duty outside Claude's door.

"Make quite sure that Mrs. Prendergast doesn't go into Mr. Prendergast's room," Roger ordered.

"Yes, sir."

"Did Inspector Lampard leave anyone with you?"

"Two in the grounds, sir, and one in the kitchen."

"Good." Roger went down, and gave the kitchen-policeman orders to watch Maisie Prendergast's room, then beckoned Janet. She was still in the hall.

"I know what you want to do," he said. "Pop into Maisie's room and find out what she's doing. Okay. I suspect crocodile tears."

Harrington, smoking his pipe, was leaning back in an easy chair, long legs crossed at the ankles. He looked sideways at Roger. His mouth was twisted into a droll kind of smile.

"Amused?" asked Roger.

Harrington removed his pipe.

"The lady came for cursing. In a way I am amused. The situation certainly has its humour. Do you think I murdered all the Prendergasts?"

"There's a live one upstairs."

"And a drunken one as well. I did not kill any Prendergast."

"That's good."

"Were they murdered?"

"Not officially. Yet."

"Do you think they were?"

"It wouldn't surprise me."

"It wouldn't surprise anybody if Maisie and Claude were bumped off just for being themselves," Harrington said drily. He stood up. He was very tall and seemed even more powerful-looking. An odd word came to Roger's mind: sinister.

Janet came in. The way Harrington looked at her was not even remotely sinister; he was just a man.

"Hallo," she said. "Are you getting to know one another? Roger, are we going home tonight? I'm worried about Omen."

"Who?"

"The kitten who started this."

Roger grinned. "The girl who didn't believe in omens! He'll be warm enough, and he won't starve if I remember that delicate way you balanced the saucer on the milk jug. I doubt if we'll get home tonight. It's half-past eleven. It depends on when Dr. Tenby returns."

"Are *you* staying the night, Mr. Harrington?" Janet asked innocently.

"I'm going home," announced Harrington. "My address is 42, Hill Mansions, Kingston-on-Thames. If you want me after eight-thirty in the morning you'll find me at Deans Court Road, where I work for my living. Good-night." He went out abruptly.

"Is it my imagination, or have you annoyed him?" Janet asked.

"I wouldn't like to say. How is Maisie?"

"I didn't hear a sound when I listened at her door, and she wasn't crying when I went in, she was looking at herself in the mirror. When she caught sight of me, she began to boo-hoo. Her scarf and the collar of her coat, at the front, are damp. It isn't raining, and she didn't cry all that number of tears."

"Odour?"

"Of whisky. She was putting on an act, she wasn't drunk. You thought of that, didn't you? You're quite bright sometimes. Why on earth come here and hurl suspicions at Harrington's *bona fides*, darling? No one in their right senses would take any notice of what she said."

"That's what Harrington said, but he may not be right. Lampard will watch Harrington, though, and when the time comes we'll talk to Maisie. Can you sleep in a chair?"

"That pet Petrie has aired a bed in a spare room," Janet said. "If only that kitten—"

She broke off, when Roger grinned at her.

"You can turn in, sweet."

"Nothing would make me undress tonight, but I will go and lie down. Roger—"

"Yes?"

"Do you suspect Harrington?"

"Not of tonight's crimes."

"Of anything?"

"Did Maisie say any more about him?"

"No. She seemed almost sorry for her outburst."

"Before I suspect him I want to know more about him," Roger said. "We'll get the Yard busy in the morning. In fact I'll get 'em busy on some things now. Off you go."

He gave her a hug and a kiss, and she went out. Suddenly, he opened the door; she was near the foot of the stairs.

"Hi!"

"Roger! You scared me." She swung round.

"Where's this room?" he demanded.

"Just along the passage to the right."

"So long as I know," he said. "I think we'll go up to see Mark."

Mark was still unconscious, but his colour was better, and his breathing was more normal. Janet went into a small bedroom which had a huge double bed. Roger left her.

When Tenby called, he said that Mark would wake up with nothing worse than a headache. His report on Claude was also encouraging. Claude might be expected to recover, although he would not be up and about again for some days.

"Can you say any more about the cause of the attack?"

"Symptoms are of barbiturate poisoning, but I'll need to check. Don't hold it against me if I'm wrong."

Roger called the Yard when Tenby had gone. Abie Fenton had been missing from his usual haunts for three days, he was told, and there was no trace of his recent London movements. Charlie Clay had evaded the policeman who had been watching him; he had last been seen in the vicinity of Putney.

Lampard rang to say that Harrington had gone straight home, and that Abie Fenton's body was now at the Guilford Morgue, and the inquest would be held in forty-eight hours unless Roger had any reason for wanting it earlier or later.

"No, that will do," said Roger. "I'm going to stay the night in case of more trouble. I want to talk to Claude if he comes round, too."

"I certainly should," approved Lampard. "You can rely on my men. They have orders to take your instructions."

"Thanks very much," said Roger warmly. "Lampard," he informed Janet a little later, "is much better than I expected. And he shares one fear."

"What's that?"

"That there might be more trouble here."

Petrie had "found" some accessories, including toothbrushes and pyjamas. Janet went to see Maisie again before going to bed, and found her already asleep, or pretending to be.

Roger waited up until two o'clock, then went upstairs again. Janet, wearing her slip, belt and panties, looked lost and desirable in the huge bed.

Roger undressed to his underclothes, and got in beside her. He soon dozed off . . .

He was awakened by Petrie bearing a tray with morning tea. Roger struggled up.

"Quiet night, Petrie?"

"Very quiet, sir. It appears to have been quite uneventful everywhere." Petrie evidently saw that as a matter to be thankful for. "Your friend is much better, sir."

While Janet sipped tea, Roger hurried into Mark's room, Mark was sitting up on pillows, and a cup of tea was in his right hand. His bandage was fixed in such a way that it half-covered his right eye. The other eye looked heavy and bloodshot, but his lips were curved in sardonic amusement at his own plight. He had been awake for some time, and that had helped him to see everything in the right perspective. He knew nothing more than he had last night.

"I'll go back to town and brood over my china," he said. "A child should have known I was being lured away. Any idea why?"

"You might have been taken for someone else," Roger suggested.

"Such as?"

"Such as Harrington."

"Who might not have escaped so lightly," Mark remarked. "Too much guesswork in this, though. By the way, did Pep Morgan bring you a message for me?"

Roger handed over the letter.

"Not bad," said Mark, when he had read it. "Potter has some scheme for the *Dreem* motley *in toto*. There's big money in *Dreem*, and money takes some beating. You'll get on to this pair as soon as you can, I suppose?"

"I will," said Roger.

By midday Mark had returned to his flat, where he intended to spend a quiet day, and Roger, having dropped Janet at home, had reached his office at the Yard, where he immediately began to collate information about the directors of *Dreem*. No news had come in, unless the fact that Potter had returned to his London house just after eleven o'clock on the previous night was news.

Lampard telephoned just after two o'clock. He had the names and addresses of seven householders in the area of the silver sand; he had cut out the cottagers and the native population, concentrating on those people who owned the larger country houses. Roger made a note, but felt no surprise or emotion of any kind until Lampard said:

"Finally—Martin Transom, Yew House, Delaware."

"Transom!" exclaimed Roger.

"A director of *Dreem*," said Lampard, drily. "Didn't you know he lived there?"

"I did not," said Roger.

Lampard made no comment, and rang off. Roger pondered the best way of getting information from the *Dreem* directors and about their business with Gabriel Potter.

He concentrated on background details about the directors

themselves. He found that only McFallen had any social pretensions. He was reputedly happily married, childless, entertained on a big scale. Transom also said to be happily married, had two children, one a daughter named Garielle. Widdison was a bachelor, Hauteby a widower.

Roger thought: Garielle Transom means something. He could get no information from the Yard, and telephoned the *Daily Echo*. That national daily's social editor, a mournful man who could get little space for social items, was only too ready to talk.

"Garielle Transom?" he echoed. "Yes, debutante in 1939. Nice looking girl. Father's got pots of money, one of the *Dreem* people, you know. Garielle lit out of the family just after the war began and joined one of the women's services, ATS I think. No, wait a minute—" the rustling of papers sounded over the telephone. "The WAAFs. Had a bit of a fandoogle with her family about it, and apparently didn't tell them what she was doing. They made a hue-and-cry about her, and discovered her eventually in RAF blue. That was when newspapers were papers, not War sheets. Eh . . . Oh, yes, reunion all right. All a happy family again. I suppose I can't ask you why you want to know?"

"Later," said Roger firmly. "Many thanks." He rang off and almost at once called the *Echo* again and asked for a photograph of Garielle Transom and her family, and McFallen's as well.

He collected the photographs, and found that the social editor had been jaundiced; Garielle Transom was not simply pretty, she had something exceptional in the way of looks.

"Sergeant from Guildford called," Eddie Day said when Roger returned. "Says he'll call again."

The sergeant had a report on Harrington. He worked in a small rubber factory at Kingston, and the factory's work was extremely hush-hush, for it manufactured new fittings for a secret aircraft. Harrington was the owner of the company. Before the war it had been unknown, but Government contracts had made it a flourishing concern. Harrington was industrious, and apparently dedicated to his job. He spent most of his evenings at home, but occasionally had a visitor, always the same attractive young woman. Harrington's neighbours hinted that they did not approve of a bachelor having a young woman at his flat. The girl, who was in the WAAFs, always left about ten o'clock.

"In the WAAFs," mused Roger, when he received the report. He thought of Garielle Transom, and decided that he was at the dangerous game of jumping to conclusions. But he was restless.

Potter had been at his office all day, and Lampard reported from Guildford that at Delaware Mrs. Prendergast had stayed in her room, while Claude was gradually improving.

He telephoned Janet, said he was going to see Harrington at Kingston but should be back by eight. Janet said she hoped he would be, because the kitten missed him badly. Chuckling, Roger went downstairs and drove to Kingston, finding Hill Mansions after some little trouble, in a road turning off Kingston Hill.

He went up to the first floor and rang the bell.

A girl in WAAF uniform answered his ring. It was Garielle Transom. Roger recognized her at once as the original of the photograph from the *Echo*.

10

GARIELLE

"Good evening," said Garielle Transom.

"Is Mr. Harrington in, please?" Roger asked, trying to hide his surprise.

"Not at the moment, but he usually gets in about half-past six," said Garielle. "Can I give him a message?"

"I'll wait, if I may." Roger hesitated and said nothing more until she stepped aside for him to enter a tiny hall which appeared to have no furniture but a rug and a hat-stand. "My name is West. Roger West."

Garielle appeared disinterested; he watched for any reaction which might suggest that Harrington had talked to her of the happenings at Delaware, but if she had heard of Roger West before she didn't say so.

"If you'll wait in here," she said, "I'll tell him as soon as he comes in. You'll have to excuse me, I'm preparing supper."

She smiled; her blue eyes were lovely.

For some minutes he did no more than look at the deep crimson paint of the door of the room into which she had shown him. The fact that it had once flashed through his mind that the WAAF visitor might be Garielle Transom had made the encounter more of a shock.

He lowered himself to an easy chair. It was so well sprung and deep that he went further than he expected and hit his head against the back, which was soft and yielding; a chair made for comfort and nothing else.

The room was large, and the far end held a dining table, sideboard, and four chairs.

There were no pictures on the walls, but there were three delicately painted masks, all women's faces. The outlines were thin and severe, there was no beauty in them except the colouring; this was a place for Mark rather than Roger. In one corner of the lounge was a baby grand, in inlaid walnut; the general effect was one of luxuriousness. The rest of the furniture was also of inlaid walnut. The radiogram in the corner nearest the fireplace was what a salesman could say with honesty was a "handsome piece."

Two vases on the mantelpiece made Roger widen his eyes; through Mark, he knew enough about pottery and china to know that they were no ordinary pieces.

A set of bookshelves on one side of the fireplace was equally instructive. A leather-bound set of Conrad was almost the only approach to anything light. There were some text-books on rubber; there was a Livy, a *Rise and Fall*, *Seven Pillars of Wisdom*.

Roger was looking at these when the door swung open, and Harrington appeared. His face was set.

"What the hell are you doing here?" he demanded with angry deliberation.

Roger said: "*A là* Maisie Prendergast? What have *you* been drinking? Absinthe?"

"I've no time to waste with you. I don't propose to be harried by you or all the policemen at Scotland Yard. I've had too many asking questions at my factory as it is. What *do* you want?"

"Finding out that you and Miss Transom were acquainted was only a matter of time. Why be so upset?"

"That's my business."

"And *Dreem* business."

Harrington glowered; his hands were bunched by his sides.

Roger passed him. Garielle Transom approached from another room. He could smell cooking bacon.

He admired the grace with which the girl walked. She unfastened a towel from her waist, one that had served as an apron.

"Bill," she began, "don't you think——?

"No, I don't," growled Harrington. "I've had enough of the blasted police force. They've been watching me all day, putting impertinent questions to my workers and neighbours, and generally asking for a pain in the neck. If West doesn't make himself scarce quickly, he's going to get one."

"Not a pain in my neck," said Roger. "Just a headache thinking about you." It was cheap but might make Harrington worry, later. He inclined his head to Garielle, and went out by the front door. He had a feeling that Harrington was urged to kick him, but he forced himself to make a decorous exit, and did not look round when he reached the landing of the staircase.

The door banged. Harrington seemed much more upset than police investigation justified. He must have known that they would check.

Roger whistled under his breath as he went into the street. A man was walking along it, also whistling; Roger approached him, and said:

"I'm Inspector West."

"Yes, sir." Big brown eyes were on Roger. "Detective Sergeant Colton of Kingston, sir." It was Colton who had telephoned.

"How long will it take you to get another man here?" Roger asked.

"About fifteen to twenty minutes, if I telephoned. Or perhaps it would be better if you phoned. There's a kiosk at the next corner."

"You phone," said Roger. "Say that I've asked for it." He watched the CID man go along the street, and glanced up at Harrington's flat. The curtains were pulled aside, and Harrington was looking out. Roger fancied that he saw the girl by his side.

Roger strolled past.

He waited at a corner until the reinforcements arrived from Kingston. One man he detailed to watch Harrington, the other the girl who, the first detective told him, had arrived at about half-past three. He was reminded that it was not going to be easy in the black-out.

"Do the best you can," Roger said, and walked briskly towards Kingston Hill.

Harrington was no longer looking out of the window. Roger started to whistle again, and eyed the kiosk on the corner of the next street. He felt that he needed more information about the Transoms, and particularly on how Harrington stood in relation to them. He did not believe that Harrington was ignorant of Garielle's identity, and there was no apparent reason why he should not have told of his association with a member of a *Dreem* family on the previous night.

Roger entered the kiosk and rang up Sergeant Sloane, asking him to find out how Harrington stood with the Transoms. He was concentrating on this, and did not notice the man who approached the kiosk slowly. A man who had come from Hill Mansions Road, with a muffler well about his neck and wearing a large hat; it was too large, and had a very wide brim. A dozen people had passed the kiosk, but this man was obviously making for it.

"Yes, ring me at Fulham," Roger said, and rang off.

The large hat filled his immediate vision, and the owner of it opened the kiosk door. Roger doubled his fist instinctively, and then saw an eye peering at him from beneath the brim, a bloodshot but humorous, familiar eye.

"Hold it," implored Lessing.

Roger stepped on to the pavement, took Mark's arm, and led him away.

"Why the swaddling clothes? Aren't you supposed to be resting in your little flat?"

"I was tempted," admitted Mark. His other eye appeared. He

had dispensed with bandages and was managing with sticking plaster. He had a headache, he said, but nothing else. "I wanted to see more of Harrington."

"Wrapped up like an imitation Texan," jeered Roger. "You could have been knocked into the middle of next week. Harrington doesn't want visitors tonight."

"So I guessed," said Mark. "I was in a flat opposite. I bribed a maid for a window seat. Ten shillings and my charm showed me most of what happened, although I didn't hear the bull bellowing. He did bellow, didn't he?"

"Did you see the girl?"

"I've already prepared a story that will make Janet set about you with more than the kitten," Mark said. "Who is she?"

"Garielle Transom," said Roger.

"I take it that Harrington is having an *affaire*, and objected to you muscling in?"

"Are you really as dense as you make out?"

Mark frowned. "About what? I—Good God, *Transom!*"

"The penny has dropped," said Roger sardonically. "Yes, that's Harrington's lady love, and in the words of the politicians it opens up avenues for exploration. She knows him well, she has her own key, and she was taking a housewifely interest in his supper. A matter of some interest."

Mark said: "What's the stronger word? What are you going to do?"

"All I can," said Roger. "It looks like a job for you, to begin with. I wish you hadn't been cracked over the head, you'd have been fit enough for it otherwise."

"I'm fit," asserted Mark. "What do you know about Garielle and her family?"

Roger told him what little he knew.

By then they had reached Roger's car which was parked close by.

"Which way are you going?" Roger asked.

"Delaware Village," replied Mark. "Then to Yew House, and

the Transom *ménage*. I've evolved a very convincing story," he added with a grin. "I am working for a solicitor acting on behalf of an unnamed relative of the Prendergasts. No names, professional etiquette and all that. The relative is worried because of the possibility of murder, and wonders if so-and-so could give him any information. Such as, were any of the family of P. worried before their death. The idea," added Mark, "was evolved before I knew of Garielle. I'd thought of looking up each of the *Dreem* directors. You don't want to do that officially yet, do you?"

"No," said Roger. "You be careful, and report after each visit."

"You shall have a report whenever I get one. Or if. I'm told by a friend of a friend that Widdison is a terrifying old bird, McFallen a gay Scot with a bright sense of humour and a love of whisky, and Hauteby a man of flint. He's younger than the others, and obsessed by business. He combines the duties of secretary and general manager of *Dreem*, hence his position on the board. A protegé of Septimus P., I gather."

"Tackle him carefully," said Roger. "And in case you forget, *I* don't know what's in your mind. There's another thing," Roger went on. "Why are these directors so interested in Potter? Two of them are, anyhow."

"Another thing?" echoed Mark. "I thought that was the same one. Give me a lift into Kingston, will you?" he added. "I'm so hard up for petrol I daren't chase around for Harrington in the car, and had to take a taxi. If you happen to have a spare coupon—"

Roger grinned. "I'll see what I can do tomorrow."

Half an hour later Roger, having dropped Mark in Kingston to pick up his own car, drove into the garage of his house, the doors of the garage being open, and then went in the back way.

The kitten arched its back cautiously against his legs.

"Hallo, Omen," said Roger. "You're improving." He whistled, and shouted: "Half-past seven and I'm home." There was no answer, and he frowned as he went into the lounge, then mounted the stairs two at a time and searched the three bedrooms and the bathroom. He called: "Jan, where are you?"

The kitten began to purr against his legs.

"This is nothing to celebrate," said Roger. "Where is she? Next door, I suppose, and I don't want half-an-hour's chat with the Featherbys. You couldn't take a message for me, could you? No, I thought not." He lit a cigarette and stared reproachfully at the closed door of the kitchen, absurdly put out that Janet was not there to meet him. He laughed suddenly, remembering the lonely hours she had spent here recently, and reminding himself that she was not due back until eight o'clock—or at least did not expect him until then.

The telephone made him jump.

"That'll be her," he said, and lifted the receiver eagerly, to be greeted by a man's deep voice, and feel astonishingly disappointed.

"That you West?" asked the voice, and went on: "It's Simmonds, here, of AY Division. I thought I'd better ring you." Simmonds was a divisional superintendent. "The thing is," he went on, "that your wife has had an accident, West . . . no, nothing very serious, a bit of concussion. She's at the Memorial Hospital. Oh, that's all right, goodnight."

• • • •

Accident, thought Roger, his heart thumping. How on earth could it have happened? Where had she been? What had happened to her? He took the car out again after shutting the door on the kitten, which had begun a fugue in *miaow* major. Ten minutes later he was at the hospital; in twelve he was being reassured by a matron.

"She's perfectly all right, Mr. West. It will be wise for her to stay here for the night, as we're not in any hurry for the bed, and she'll be better if she doesn't get up. Slight concussion, perhaps, but little more than a severe shaking."

Roger felt weak with relief.

He was led to the ward where some dozen patients were in bed. Janet was near the door. Her face lit up when he entered.

"I wondered if they'd let you in," she said after he had kissed her. "I kept emphasising the fact that you're a policeman, and I expect it worked. I was such a fool! I'd meant to make some scones, but Mrs. Featherby came in and I didn't have time. I thought the shop on the corner might have some. I just walked right into the car."

Roger said: "You did, did you? At the end of the street?"

"Yes, opposite the shop. I thought I heard a *miaow* and looked round as I stepped off the kerb, you know how it is sometimes." Janet was too excited, her eyes were over-bright and she had a slight flush. "I saw it and jumped back. I didn't actually get hit, that's the absurd thing. But I banged my head on the kerb. I know what Mark felt like last night now!"

"I wish you didn't," said Roger.

"Are you home for the evening?"

"Yes." As soon as he said it he wished he had said "no."

"It would happen," mourned Janet. "I was going to come home, but they persuaded me to stay here. I'm not very steady on my legs. Can you spend the evening with Mark?"

"I shall," Roger promised her. "But you—"

"I'll be all right, and the nurse is a dear. You don't mind me staying? I mean, if you'd rather I came home, I will."

"Forget it," smiled Roger. "I'm so relieved it's no worse that I shall probably open a tin of sardines for Quisling."

"Who?"

"Quisling is Omen's new name," said Roger firmly. "His *miaow* did the damage, didn't it? The Fifth column." He stayed for ten minutes, telling her a little about the events of the day.

Then the matron told him that he would have to leave, as the patients were being prepared for the night. As it was a comparatively mild injury, perhaps it was not worth transferring Mrs. West to a private ward.

"It certainly isn't," said Janet.

"No," agreed Roger.

"Accident," he murmured as he entered the narrow thorough-fare in which the hospital was situated. "I wonder." He drove to the Divisional Headquarters, and was soon sitting opposite the large slow-moving Superintendent Simmonds. Simmonds had three chins and a pendulous nose.

"Yes," he answered, "one of my men was nearby when it happened, and took the number of the car, which didn't stop. It was an old Buick. He says that the car was parked at the corner, and the driver jumped in quickly when he saw Mrs. West coming. That's in his own words."

"I was all kinds of a damned fool for ever letting Janet go with me last night," Roger said.

He talked freely to Simmonds, a wily old policeman who had often advised him and, because they were not together at the Yard, was less affected by rank superiority. Simmonds listened attentively, occasionally rubbing the bridge of his long, wriggly nose and, when Roger had finished, said:

"Potter's in this up to his adam's apple. He's been as deep a dozen times before, and he's always fooled us, but he'll miss his step one day and there's no reason why you shouldn't be at hand to pick him up. Chatworth would be tickled to death. Another wily old bird, our Chatworth! He knows you and Lessing are as thick as thieves, and he also knows that if Potter's to be tripped up it will have to be unprofessionally. He thinks Lessing will take a chance. He wants Potter or he wouldn't have given you the go-ahead. But Potter knows it as well as you do, and if you ask me, he's playing for big stakes. Don't ask me how I know, ask yourself."

"Could be," said Roger.

"Talkative, aren't you?" remarked Simmonds sarcastically. "You see what I mean?"

"Yes. Thanks."

"Don't thank me," Simmonds implored. "I'm just shooting my

mouth off. I'll tell a man or two to keep a special eye on Bell Road. You could just pass the hint to Janet that she should watch her step. Don't want to scare her too much, but with Potter—"

Roger left, reassured on one point, worried on another. This was Potter's work. Potter used Clay, Potter had probably arranged Fenton's murder, Potter might be working Maisie-Claude-Harrington. Certainly Potter was pulling a lot of strings and making the puppets dance.

Roger remembered the impact of the car on Fenton's body, and could picture Janet being run down. He clenched his teeth.

The kitten *miaowed* plaintively, but spurned a saucer of milk. Instead, it followed him into the lounge, where there was no fire, and jumped onto his knee. It curled itself and purred contentedly, while Roger developed a headache.

It was half-past ten before he reminded himself that he had not eaten since lunch time, and he was brewing a cup of tea after a snack supper, commiserating with himself while thinking that Janet must find it much lonelier than he had realized, when the front door bell rang.

Mark came in.

His entry was remarkable for its silence; there was no hint of high spirits.

"Well, what?" asked Roger.

"Not nice, Roger," he said. "Nothing's nice."

"Is Transom—"

"Transom's all right," said Mark. "I was there when McFallen called to see him tonight. McFallen lives at Epsom, and they attend to *Dreem* business at their respective homes, over dinner and cigars. McFallen didn't stay long, but left a message that put Transom's wind right up. He didn't say so but it showed. Then McFallen drove away. There's a nasty bend just past Transom's place, and if you go off the road you go over an edge into a sand quarry about seventy yards down. A sheer drop. We heard the crash from Transom's window. I got there first. Not at all nice," repeated Mark. "His pieces are being looked after by Lampard, who is also examining the car. McFallen drove himself, a Rolls-Royce. What's the betting that there won't be another *death by misadventure* verdict?"

"You'd better have a drink," Roger said. He felt cold when he thought of Janet.

He poured two whiskies and soda.

"Thanks," Mark said. "Well, I decided I'd be clever, and visit McFallen's wife. A nice, dumpy little Scots woman. I don't like thinking about her face when I told her that her husband was dead. Have you ever seen anyone's heart break in front of you? My God, we've got to stop this."

"Yes," said Roger, dry-mouthed. "What about Transom?" he asked. "Apart from closing up after McFallen had called, did he give you anything to bite on?"

"He told me politely that he knew of no surviving relative of the Prendergasts, and that he was quite satisfied with the way the police had handled the necessary inquiries." Mark's voice remained his own, but his manner grew faintly pompous, his words took on a rotundity which Roger was sure was an excellent mimicry of Arthur Transom. The whisky was doing him good. "He was, of course, quite prepared and happy to meet my claimant in person, and would be delighted to offer any assistance once he had met him." Mark smiled unexpectedly. "In other words he called me a liar, but he was worried. He had that look in the eyes. He also gave me the impression that my visit wasn't the thing which started the worry; Mr. Transom has something on his mind. McFallen shared it, and I think McFallen had taken news which was not good to Transom. The effect was instantaneous, but all I got out of it was that Transom 'would be there.' Time and date of the presumed meeting wasn't specified, and McFallen went off, as I've said."

"You didn't think it worth while watching Transom and leaving Mrs. McFallen?"

Mark glowered.

"What is this, a lesson in ABC? I had phoned Pep Morgan earlier in the day, and he was watching Transom for me. I couldn't have done much anyhow, without more petrol. The McFallen house was on my way home." He sat down in an easy chair, stretched his legs and scratched the kitten under the chin. It purred like an aero-engine. "Where's Janet?"

Roger began to explain.

"My God," Mark said. "That's terrifying."

His eyes showed consternation. He was silent when Roger finished.

"Yes, terrifying. It looks as if Potter sent me a reminder that Janet's vulnerable, too. Always assuming that it is Potter. Someone is certainly very anxious to get me off the hunt. And you, too."

"He doesn't give a damn about me."

"Well, I wouldn't blame him," admitted Roger. "But where's the evidence?"

"In front of you. To a past master in the arranging of accidents, I was an easy victim last night. Think of the hills in that part of Surrey. I could have "fallen" down a dozen and broken my neck, and no one would have been any the wiser. I didn't because our Potter—*I* say it's Potter—reckoned that I was no serious liability. In fact Potter probably decided that it was wiser to let me play around, because—"

He stopped.

"Go on," said Roger.

"Just an idea," said Mark. "Vague and improbable, anyhow. I mean, Potter knows I'm looking for something, and thought I had it at the flat, or he wouldn't have sent Charlie. He probably thinks I'm still looking for it. He also wants it badly."

"A bit involved, but I follow you. I wonder if he could have suspected that this thing he wants badly—if it's he, and if he wants something badly!—was at Delaware House. There might have been no reason for the call on you except to get us thinking along the wrong lines. That's a possibility as great as your idea.

We'll keep 'em both in mind. Now what about a concentrated effort? I'll keep at Harrington, you keep at the Tramsoms, and we'll compare notes tomorrow. All right?"

"Yes," said Mark. At that moment the telephone bell rang. Mark lifted the receiver—"Oh it's you, Pep," he said. "What's happened?"

"I've been trying to get you all the evening," said Morgan. "I thought you'd like to know that there are others at Transom's house. Widdison and Hauteby, as a matter of fact. And I'm getting cold."

"How long have they been there?" Mark demanded.

"Hauteby's only just arrived. Are you coming out here?"

"If I can," said Mark, and put a hand over the mouthpiece as he turned to Roger. "Petrol," he said imploringly. "Petrol. A matter of life or death. Can you spare a couple of gallons?"

"There's a can in the garage."

"Bless your heart!" Mark uncovered the receiver. "All right, Pep, I'll be there in about an hour."

He rang off, and held out a hand for the garage key.

"One can, I said, and one can you'll get," said Roger. "I'll come and superintend. I think I'll come with you all the way, too," he added as he reached the kitchen door.

The telephone rang again. Roger handed Mark the key, and went back into the lounge. Detective Sergeant Sloane thought that Mr. West ought to know that Chief Inspector Lampard of Guildford had telephoned for him, and obtained his private number. Roger replaced the receiver, and contemplated the kitten.

He was still tempted to go with Mark, but it might be wise to allow Mark and Morgan to work by themselves; they would be freer without him. He held no illusions; knew that Mark would use the law as he thought it should be used, and ignore its finer points whenever he considered it necessary.

Mark was outside for ten minutes, and the telephone kept silent. Mark returned with his hands oily, and a smear of dirt on his right cheek.

"Thanks for your help," he said sarcastically. "I hope you have to empty a can of petrol in the blackout tomorrow night. Are you coming?"

"Lampard's going to telephone in a few minutes. I expect he wants to tell me about McFallen. Good hunting, Mark."

Very slowly and appreciatively, Mark Lessing smiled.

"Thanks," he said, and went away.

When he had gone, Roger felt heavy-hearted and deeply anxious. The injury to Janet, the excess of violence, the darkening mystery, crowded into his mind. There were a dozen things he wanted to do, but as a policeman he could do few of them. In Mark's place he could tackle Harrington, for instance, and even Potter again, but—what made him think he could do better than Mark?

Mark was running into danger.

It was a strange, half-way position for Roger. If the police took all the official action they could, it might lead nowhere and could scare off the criminals for a time, but only for a time. By going into this almost alone, with some help from Pep Morgan, Mark was sticking his neck right out. True, Mark wanted to; equally true, Chatworth saw the value to the police. But he, Roger West, saw the acute danger to his friend, and ached to be in his place, or at least sharing it with him.

It was close on midnight when Lampard called, to talk of the McFallen "accident." He felt that Roger should know that there were suspicions that the steering-column of McFallen's Rolls-Royce had been tampered with, but nothing more than suspicions. Lampard wondered whether West considered it wise to watch Transom's house.

At least he could help Mark this way.

"At the moment, I don't see why," said Roger thoughtfully. "Lessing has been telling me about it. I gather that McFallen's car wasn't at Yew House long enough to be tampered with, so the damage was done before McFallen started his journey." He did not ask why Lampard had taken the extraordinary step of asking his advice, but suspected there was a catch in the Guilford man's question.

"Lessing's there, is he?" said Lampard drily. "Is he better?"

"Much."

"All right." Lampard was suddenly brisk again. "I'll do nothing for tonight."

Roger replaced the receiver and regarded the kitten with his head on one side.

"Quisling," he observed, "Lampard's a deep 'un. Was Mark at Transom's, that was his question. Does he also think that Mark might learn something we can't, or is he going to surround the blasted house so that if Mark does what he shouldn't, there'll be trouble. Lampard wouldn't do that on us, would he?"

The kitten cleaned the inside of a hind leg earnestly.

"There are times when I wish I could take Mark's advice and get out of the Force," went on Roger. "I would be able to move more freely. But on the other hand . . ."

He went to bed and was asleep by one o'clock, and awoke soon after seven-thirty. He lay for some time in the pleasant and drowsy stage between sleeping and waking, then realized that he was alone, and wondered whether Janet was up yet. He must ring through to find what time she would be home; it would be much better if he could be here. Or better still, if he went to fetch her. There was no news from Mark, then. He rang Mark's flat to find the number engaged; Mark would probably ring him soon.

He washed, shaved, got breakfast, allowed himself Janet's share of bacon as well as his own, and found himself wondering where Mark was, and what Mark had done in the past nine hours. At nine o'clock there was no message. He began to feel annoyed. He telephoned the hospital, to learn that Janet was not leaving until three o'clock in the afternoon, but she had had a sound night's sleep and was much better. He tried Mark's number and was told there was no reply. He waited for about twenty minutes, and then decided that he could stay away from the Yard no longer.

When he reached his office only Eddie Day was there, engrossed in some bank notes which few people could have distinguished from the genuine article; he explained at great length how cleverly he had traced the flaw in him. Other DIs came in and out. Roger was on edge since there was still no news from Mark, but he displayed a polite interest; Eddie took a childish pleasure in his triumphs.

At half-past twelve a uniformed policeman came in, to tell Roger that a Miss Garielle Transom had called, and could she see him?

11

MEETING AT YEW HOUSE

Mark Lessing, meanwhile, disliked his night drive to Yew House.

No one but a fool would think that there was any real chance of getting to the house in time to find the three *Dreem* directors together. No one but a greater fool would have imagined that he could do anything even if he found them. No one but a fool—

A car approaching without lights nearly crashed into him. He flickered his own headlamps feverishly. The light was not good, although the beam of his headlamps allowed him to make fair speed.

He brooded on his position at the Ministry of Information. He had tried to resign three times and been told that he was doing an essential war job; the Powers that Were had strange ideas on what was essential. He was having a "four-day-free" spell then, but was due back at the office the day after tomorrow, when he would be on duty for four days in succession.

"I'll apply for leave," he decided. "I haven't had any since Christmas."

He reached the drive of Yew House at one o'clock, and congratulated himself on making the run in little over an hour. But he still felt sure that he was too late, that Morgan would have gone or at best be in an evil temper. He could hardly blame Morgan, who—

"That you, Mr. Lessing?"

In spite of the faint reflection of light from the headlamp, Morgan's teeth glistened. It needed only a little imagination to see his twinkling, high-polished shoes. His voice was not gruff or gloomy or irritable but held a hint of excitement and tension. Mark wound down a window swiftly.

"Yes, Pep. How are tricks?"

"They're still here," reported Morgan. "No one's come out, but I'll give you three guesses as to who's gone in."

"Potter," sighed Mark.

"Potter it is! He arrived just after I'd telephoned. It's a lucky thing he wasn't a bit sooner or I would have missed him while I was phoning in the village. Potter," repeated Morgan in a whisper, "and Transom, Widdison, and Hauteby. Peculiar thing, Mr. Lessing, don't you think?"

"I believe you've been thinking a lot about this affair, Pep. Yes, it's peculiar. Do you know what room they're in?"

"One upstairs," said Pep promptly. "The only room where there's a light. I can just see a chink, close to the house. The corner room, on the right side. I don't think that anyone is up, apart from those four. There was a light in the kitchen up to midnight, I saw it through the keyhole. It's out now."

"Well, well," Mark said. "I would like to know what they're talking about, wouldn't you?"

"I certainly would," agreed Morgan. "But you know me, Mr. Lessing. I can't go outside the law, but I can hang around and give you a whistle if anyone else came along. Mr. West didn't come with you, I see."

"No. What's the front door like?"

Morgan thought it was a bit of a teaser, and he could assure Mr. Lessing that none of the downstairs windows was open, although it might be possible to push aside the catch of one or two of them. All the windows were of the old-fashioned sash-cord type. The trouble was that they probably squeaked.

"I'll try the front door," decided Mark.

He did not ask himself what would happen if he were caught;

he relied on making a quick getaway in an emergency, and on his plausibility to explain himself satisfactorily if things went wrong.

He worked at the front door, and saw a picture of Transom in his mind's eye. A big, portly man, good-looking although with a fleshy jowl. Pale-faced, with wide, large grey eyes, grey hair and a close-clipped grey moustache. A short, straight nose, rather wide at the nostrils, and well-marked lips. A man with a presence, less pompous than portentous.

Mark felt the barrel of the lock moving.

He wore gloves, and manipulated the key dextrously. He had practised a great deal and been schooled at one time by a reformed cracksman who, in his heyday, had been at least the rival of Charlie Clay and Abie Fenton.

"Got it?" asked Morgan.

"Yes." The door eased open as Mark pushed, and a faint glow of light showed.

"I'll be seeing you," said Morgan. "One good blow on the old whistle if there's any cause for alarm."

He went swiftly back along the drive to the gates. His car was parked some distance away, and Mark knew that if he were seen by the police he would swear that he was watching the outside of the house only, for a client whom he would not name.

Mark was relieved when he realized that the hall floor was covered from wall to wall with carpet; the stairs and the passages were likely to be, too. The dim light came not from the electric chandelier above his head, but from a tiny oil lamp burning on a table where there were several magazines. It was less hall than lounge, stretching the full depth of the house, furnished with easy chairs and sofas. A big fireplace took up a large portion of one wall, and on either side of it was a suit of armour, complete with broad-sword. Above them, two large oil paintings loomed dark and shadowy. The hall was panelled throughout in dark oak, heavy but impressive.

Some whim of the architect had set the staircase leading from the left of the hall, to a wide landing and then a gallery. Looking upwards, Mark saw the dark void of the ceiling, more like the nave of a church than the ceiling of the hall of a private house. Transom did things in style.

Mark went upstairs.

There was a faint murmuring sound in the quiet of the hall; someone was talking. His heart beat fast when, on the top stair, he saw a sliver of light coming from beneath a door on the right of the gallery, which was also carpeted. He approached it swiftly, while the muttering grew louder.

It was Potter's voice.

Mark put his right hand to his pocket, and reached the door. Potter's words were just distinguishable.

"I am sorry, gentlemen, but I have endeavoured to make this suggestion a practical one. I find the difficulties insuperable. You will, I trust—" the cold, sardonic expression in his voice had made many men squirm—"agree that I have given you an opportunity for a full discussion of your views."

Someone said: "This doesn't sound like you, Potter."

"Doesn't it, Mr. Widdison? It is me, I assure you. Is there anything else that I can do for you tonight?"

Someone said: "I'm a long way from satisfied."

"Perhaps, gentlemen, you will be able to find another solicitor more capable than I," said Potter. "Before I go, I feel it incumbent on me to express my very real sympathy for the sad loss to the board of directors in the person of Sir Andrew McFallen. Good night."

Mark stepped to one side, into shadow.

Footsteps, dull and muffled by carpet, sounded inside the room. The door opened. The sliver of light became a beam which shone uncomfortably close to Mark, who took three steps backwards, and used a doorway for cover.

Potter stepped out, a tall, thin, angular silhouette.

"I'll be back in a moment," said another man.

Transom appeared, and walked with Potter towards the

stairs. He had closed the door, and only the faint glow from the oil lamp spread any light until Transom switched on a torch. Neither man spoke as they made their way down the stairs.

Mark followed, watching them from the first landing.

The soft, padding footsteps, the absence of words, all added to the tension between Transom and Potter. That the solicitor had contrived another doublecross was the thought uppermost in Mark's mind.

The two men reached the hall.

As they crossed towards the front door Mark saw a movement towards the right, from the fireplace. He stiffened as he saw more than a movement; there was a man there—a dark-clad man, with his right arm raised and some kind of weapon in his hand.

"Look out!" Mark shouted.

The man pounced, but Mark's warning had given time for Potter to swing round, and Transom to jump forward. Both moved so swiftly that the dark-clad stranger's blow went harmlessly through the air. The force of it overbalanced him. He staggered forward a few steps, his head nodding towards the ground. Potter swerved to one side, to avoid him. Transom stood like a man transfixed.

There was a split second's silence. Mark moved then, beginning to go down the stairs as he saw the assailant recover and swing round, striking again—*at Potter*.

There was no doubt which of the two men he aimed to injure, but Potter moved with surprising speed, brushing aside the assailant's outstretched arm. There must have been more force in Potter's blow than there appeared, for the man in black went staggering to one side. But he recovered, and flung his weapon at Potter's head.

The handle struck home.

Transom jumped forward, but with less agility than that of an elephant. He doubled up as he received a punch to his stomach. His gasp echoed high into the church-like ceiling.

A gun appeared in the dark-clad man's hand.

It glinted a blue-grey. There was a yellow flash and a sharp report. Then the door at the top of the stairs opened, and Widdison and Hauteby started down, running so heavily that they shook the staircase and set the suit of armour rattling.

The bullet missed Potter but buried itself in the panelling by his head. Potter darted towards a tall piece of furniture, near the front door. The man in black slewed his gun round, and then Mark reached him. He had no time to knock his hand aside, but went forward in a sliding tackle which knocked the gunman off his balance. The second bullet smacked into the staircase. The gunman scrambled to his feet again, but the gun had fallen, and Potter was out of sight.

The man swung round and raced to the far end of the hall. Mark jumped up, ten feet behind. A door at the other end opened, letting in a draught of cold wind. The figure was a vague shape against the faint light beyond, then disappeared. The door slammed.

Mark made for the door with Hauteby and Widdison just behind him. A voice, Hauteby's, said:

"Let me get at him!"

Hauteby pushed Mark aside and raced forward. He fired twice from the gun he had picked up in the hall. The flashes did no more than illuminate a few yards of air and ground, showing no sign of the running man.

Mark sped past Hauteby, annoyed by the way he had been shouldered aside, straining his ears to catch the direction in which the man ran. He guessed that the gunman was going towards the front of the house, and turned in that direction. As he reached the drive, the bright shaft of a searchlight shed its faint glow in the heavens. Hauteby and Widdison drew near, but there was movement on the grass and in the shrubbery alongside the drive.

Mark said *sotto voce:*

"If you must move, keep on the grass."

Mark moved along the verge of the drive. A faint rustling was ahead of him, and he imagined that his quarry was heading for the road. There might be a car there, or he might be planning to get away on foot.

Morgan should be able to help.

Morgan was out of sight, but as Mark reached the gate the beams of two headlights from his Lagonda lit up the road. Against them, Mark saw Morgan as the private detective slipped to one side, into shadow. At the end of them was the dark-clad figure, taken by surprise.

Near him was a motor-cycle.

He moved towards it, crouching, but Morgan was advancing on one side and Mark on the other. The man reached the motor-cycle, straddled it, and kicked at the starter. A dull plop-plop came, nothing else. They could see him pushing desperately, but the engine only gurgled, and they were within a few yards of him before it actually started.

Mark was in front.

He could jump and stop the man, and knew that the other had to turn the cycle off the verge before he could move away. Mark was half-prepared for the other's move: he swung the machine round, and drove straight at him.

Mark dodged to one side, pushing out a hand. He touched the man's shoulder. The machine staggered. Morgan appeared on the far side, striking out. The driver lost control, and the machine piled up against the hedge.

The light from the car showed all of this.

The driver jumped from his machine to try to save himself from being carried with it, but his coat caught against the handlebars, and he crashed down.

Then, not far off, came the bark of a shot.

A rifle-shot, Mark believed; it was clear and crisp, not heavy like a revolver shot, and too loud for an automatic. It came twice. On the second, the motor-cyclist grunted, and fell heavily on his back. It might have been imagination, but Mark fancied that he saw a dark smudge on his forehead.

Morgan reached the man. "What was that?"

"Get up," Mark said urgently. "Mind yourself."

The sharpshooter could see them in the light, although the hedge threw shadows where it overhung the roadway. But there was no further shooting, no sign of the rifleman. The first people Mark saw were Hauteby, Widdison, and Transom, gathered by the drive gates.

"Are you all struck dumb?" Mark rasped at them. "Did you see him?"

Hauteby said: "We saw no one. And we want a word with you."

"One man's dead or close to it, and the killer's within a hundred yards of here," Mark said. "Still want to stop and chat?"

12

THREE, PLUS CLAUDE

They did their best, or claimed to. Their torches carved little
arcs of light about the darkness, but they found no man with a
rifle, although there were footprints in the damp earth on the
side of the road which would be useful for the police. Mark was
in two minds about what to do now; Morgan certainly would not
want to reveal himself. The three *Dreem* directors were unknown quantities.

Mark thought with a start: "Where's Potter?"

Tramson spoke in his portentous way.

"Mr. Lessing, it is time you explained something of your presence here."

"Not yet. If you'll leave your doors wide open you must expect
what you get. Where's Gabriel Potter?"

Hauteby said: "Isn't he here?"

Mark forced back a retort. He wished he could see faces instead of pale blurs, that he could examine the motor-cyclist, go
to see Potter, and telephone the police. He would have to do the
latter himself, or at least be there when Lampard arrived; there
would be too many questions. He decided to attend to the motor-
cyclist first.

"Is any one of you a doctor?" he asked.

"No," Widdison answered. He had a croaking voice, and to
look at was an ogre of a man. The darkness was kind to him.

"Will you get to the house and telephone the police," said
Mark. "And try to persuade Potter to wait for them to arrive."

He turned on his heel, wondering whether one of them would follow. None did. He was alone when he reached the motorcyclist, whose legs were held down by his machine. He could not have moved, in any case. Torchlight revealed a small hole in his forehead; it had bled very little.

The face was unfamiliar.

Out of the gloom came Morgan's voice:

"Want me any more, Mr. Lessing?"

"You get off, thanks," said Mark. "But have a glance at this chap first." He waited while Morgan obeyed. Morgan hadn't seen the dead man before, either; it was an ordinary-looking face with no special characteristics. The dark scarf which he had worn over his mouth and chin was now about his neck.

"Poor devil," said Morgan. "Okay, I'll beat it. Sure there's nothing else?"

"No need for us both to get in a jam," Mark said. "What shoes are you wearing?"

"Don't worry about me, they won't trace my shoes from prints," said Morgan. "Shall I tell Mr. West?"

"I'll do that," said Mark.

It was cold, bleak, and lonely when Morgan had gone, and Mark was surprised that none of the men from Yew House had thought it necessary to join him. They were probably in a huddle, discussing how best to answer the inevitable awkward questions. Any one of the three, as well as Potter, might have fired the shot which had killed the motor-cyclist, but he had seen no rifle. Transom might have brought one from the house, of course, but was Transom a dead shot? And was Potter?

Mark rubbed his hands to get them warm. There were strange noises in the surrounding undergrowth, and occasional distant rumbles as if heavy transport was moving on the main road, farther to the south. The searchlights swept their unplanned course about the sky, but there was no sound of aircraft.

Mark said suddenly:

"What's happening to *me?*"

He had put out his torch, but used it again to show him the position in which the dead man was lying. Then he doused it and slid a hand into the dead man's inside breast pocket. He found a wallet, and two letters. Using the torch again, he glanced at the writing on the envelopes: they were both addressed to:

David Anderson, Esq.,
c/o Harringtons, Ltd.,
Dean Park Road, Kingston-on-Thames,
Surrey.

Mark repeated the address two or three times, then drew a deep breath. He opened the letters, finding that they were both from the same woman, ordinary letters filled with ordinary items of gossip. Both ended: *"Your affectionate sister, Cora."* He replaced them in their envelopes, clumsily because he was wearing gloves, then looked through the wallet. There was an identity card with a photograph affixed; it declared that David Anderson was an employee in the Development Department of Harringtons Ltd., that he had permission to move to any part of the factory and had access to it at any time, day and night. Mark looked at the photograph just long enough to make sure that it was that of the dead man.

Mark finished looking through Anderson's pockets, finding nothing of further interest, then stood up and lit a cigarette.

Harrington's employee; was it asking too much to believe that Anderson's presence here had nothing to do with his employer? No, thought Mark, there were limits to coincidence. He felt an urgent desire to see Harrington before the police did. That was not going to be easy, for they would not lose much time once they had identified Anderson.

Mark frowned.

The only evidence of identity was in the letters and the pass. If the police did not find these, it might take them several hours, perhaps days, to identify Anderson. There was no reason at all why the wallet and envelopes should not have slipped out of his pocket.

Mark took them again, carried them to the other side of the road and dropped them in a ditch. They would be found in a thorough search, but none was possible before daylight.

He felt better. It was certainly as well that Roger had not come, but this was really *why* Roger had not; he would have had to take official action.

Mark did not know how long he had waited, but it was three o'clock before the police arrived. Lampard was not with them. Mark was pleased about that, for Lampard's austereness was, to him, no more than a cover for suspicion of interfering amateurs. The Inspector who had arrived, Wade by name, was a much more genial type, asking quite casual questions.

The police took charge of the body.

"How many people know about this?" Wade asked.

"Four more, to my knowledge," said Mark. "Who telephoned you?"

"Mr. Transom." Wade uttered the name as if it were one which called for respect. "Is that your car along there?" The lights of his own machine shone on the Lagonda.

"Yes." For the first time Mark allowed himself to dwell on his difficulties, and he did not like the look of them. How was he to explain his presence, and the fact that the car was left away from the house? His mind worked overtime, as he walked with Wade back to Yew House.

The door was open, and a servant in a dressing-gown was waiting in the hall. Transom and his friends were in the study; would the Inspector kindly go up? Wade did not discourage Mark from going with him.

The study was the kind of room to be expected there. It had an air of wealth, even of luxury. On a small table in front of the fire, which burned brightly, was a decanter and three glasses. Transom, Widdison, and Hauteby were drinking; Potter, sitting further from the fire than any of the others, was abstemious.

Transom stood up, and the others made a pretence at it.

"Don't get up, gentlemen, please," said Wade.

Potter made a sign, inviting Mark to join him. Mark did so. Potter placed his hands on the smooth arm of his chair. Wade was talking to Transom, asking trifling little questions which Mark found irritating, but he was able to take the slip of paper which Potter had covered with his hand.

Had Wade seen that manoeuvre?

Mark was startled when Transom said:

"Mr. Lessing has been invaluable, Inspector. I hardly know what we would have done without him. It was a happy chance that he called. What about a drink?" He leaned forward for the whisky.

"Not for me, thanks," said Wade.

"Thanks," said Mark.

He stood closer to the fire, eyeing Potter who gave an almost imperceptible nod. He must have an extraordinarily strong reason for making it easy for him.

Questions and answers. Transom, Widdison, and Hauteby had met to discuss a difficult legal point with Potter. Lessing had called to see Transom—no reason was given—and had stayed at Transom's invitation. They had been discussing the death of McFallen, a sad, sad, business. This second death—Transom really did not know what to say, he was completely at a loss to understand it. He had shown Potter downstairs, and . . .

From there on his story was clear and accurate. He talked of Morgan, but not by name. Mark disclaimed any knowledge of the man, or that he could give an effective description. Wade seemed satisfied, just a little too satisfied; Mark imagined he was acting as a stop-gap for Lampard, and knew it. He could almost imagine Lampard instructing the Inspector to arouse no suspicions, to deal very gently with the *Dreem* directors.

"So it appears that Mr. Potter was to have been the victim," said Wade. "Have you any idea who it could have been, Mr. Potter?"

"I am as puzzled as Mr. Transom," Potter replied. "But—" he

gave a shrug of his narrow shoulders—"I am not without my enemies. You may be aware of that."

Wade was shocked. No, he was not aware of that. He hoped that he was not making a nuisance of himself, but he would get Mr. Transom to write out a brief statement, which all of them could sign. The identity of the murdered man would be proved as soon as possible, and the police would pass on all relevant information. Mr. Transom would understand that the circumstances made it impossible not to leave men in the grounds. The rifle; for instance, might have been thrown away, and it was valuable evidence. More, the killer might come back for something. He was barely plausible, but no more.

Transom voiced no objection, and indeed was anxious to do all he could to assist the police. It was a fine show of geniality and hearty good-fellowship, not spoiled by Transom's pomposity. Then Transom hoped that Potter and Mark would stay the night, as it had grown so late.

Mark was astonished when Potter accepted the invitation.

He refused, and Wade said he could go. He shook hands all round, and left the house, the note which Potter had given him burning a hole in his pocket. He did not try to read it, even when he reached his car. He drove towards Guildford, slowing down when he saw the little group of policemen about Anderson's body. They were working just as they had worked near Abie Fenton's.

Mark drove faster after that, but had not reached Guildford before he knew that he was being followed; and he was not sure whether to fear that Wade had sent a man after him, or whether Potter had contrived it.

He only knew that he had to evade pursuit.

．　．　．　．

The driver of the pursuing car was following Mark's headlights, using only sidelights himself. The two little orbs of faint white showed in the driving mirror. It was difficult to estimate how far the car was behind; Mark imagined it to be some fifty or sixty feet. He increased his speed, but the other car kept up. He slowed down, and the other driver did, also.

"That rules out chance," Mark said. "If they'd been planning to crash me it would have been over by now. I wish I could catch a glimpse of them." He toyed with the idea of stopping and asking the other motorist for assistance he did not need. The idea grew attractive when he was on the other side of Cobham. He pulled up abruptly, stepping into the road with his arms outstretched as the other driver applied his brakes.

The vague face of a man showed against the window, and the bright light of Mark's torch revealed Chief Inspector Lampard.

"Well I'm damned!" exclaimed Mark. "Are you going up to town at this time of night?"

Lampard blinked against the light, and asked Mark to move the beam. He was affable, for him. He was going to London, but could he help Mr. Lessing? He had been grateful for the head-lamps, his own were faulty.

Mark beamed. "Too bad. D'you know, I had an idea someone was following me, and stopped to inquire. That's all. Not much use me offering you a lift, is it, although we'd save petrol."

"No, thanks," said Lampard. "Unless you would like to park your car and come with me, Mr. Lessing. We could exchange views then."

"There's nothing I'd like better, but I must get home and get some sleep. In spite of my overdose yesterday, my eyes will hardly keep open."

He raised a hand, returned to the Lagonda, and started slowly, then making a fair speed. Once he switched on his dashboard lights to check the petrol. Thanks to Roger's two gallons he was still a quarter full; he could afford a little game with Lampard.

He played it, driving straight to Chelsea, and garaging his car noisily. Lampard passed the end of the road, and then, Mark hoped, went on about other business.

Indoors Mark opened Potter's note; it was a curt request for him, Mark, to go and see him next day. He put it aside. He wished he had not to go out again, and then had an idea. He checked Harrington's number, and called it three times with the same result, and moved away from the telephone thoughtfully. On the spur of the moment he telephoned Harrington's Ltd., expecting no reply.

A man's voice said: "This is Harrington's."

"Hallo," said Mark, "Is—er—is Mr. Harrington there?"

"Yes, he is," said the operator. "But he can't come to the telephone, he's working on a break-down, and will be until morning. Can I take a message?"

"I'll call again," said Mark.

With Harrington at his factory there was less likelihood of danger to him, and Mark gave up the idea of going to Kingston. He set the alarm for nine o'clock, after deciding that it would be pointless to telephone Roger at that hour. Lampard would report the new murder to the Yard, anyhow.

Mark was not awakened by the alarm, but by the telephone. His eyes were heavy, but he saw that it was half-past seven. He stretched out his hand for the instrument.

"Hallo," he said without enthusiasm.

"Good morning," said Gabriel Potter.

"You didn't mean seven in the morning, did you?"

"No. I wanted to make sure you did not come. It is no longer convenient."

Potter rang off without another word, and Mark stared at the telephone, replaced the receiver, shrugged his shoulders, and got out of bed. He shaved and dressed slowly and then rang up Roger, to be told that the number was engaged. He could not know that it was engaged trying to call him. He replaced the receiver and it rang sharply almost before it was in position.

"Mr. Lessing." It was Pep Morgan, with a hint of excitement in his voice. "Take a tip, go and see Harrington quickly."

Morgan rang off. Everyone was abrupt and mysterious this morning.

Half-an-hour later Mark rang the bell at Harrington's flat. There was a fine drizzle of rain, and on the mat in front of the door some mudstains and what looked like oil; Harrington had returned, unless someone else had visited the flat. After a pause, Harrington opened the door, with a towel in his hand.

" 'Morning," said Mark. "I'm glad to find you up with the lark. Can you spare me a few minutes?"

"Why?" Harrington was brusque. "I'm just going to bed. I've been up all night."

"That's odd, so have I," said Mark. "I think you'll be glad that you've spared me the time." He edged into the small, barely furnished box of a hall, while Harrington grunted and pushed open the door of the lounge-cum-dining room with his knee.

"I'll be in soon," he promised.

Mark looked round the room which Roger had thought would interest him and his eyes widened when he saw the Livy, Lawrence, and Gibbons cheek by jowl in the bookshelves by the fireplace. His lips formed a soundless whistle when he caught sight of the three masks.

He was examining one when Harrington entered, and he said with real excitement: "Harrington, that's a piece by le Fleur, isn't it?"

"It is," said Harrington. "And this is a piece by Harrington. What do you want?" He was aggressive, but not so angry as he had been with Roger.

Mark looked away from the mask.

"To play ball with you," he said. "I'm not a policeman. Hasn't that fact registered?"

"You're tarred with their brush," said Harrington. "You are all a lot of prying busybodies. If I had more time I'd gun for you, but I haven't. If you've come to tell me you're not a policeman, good morning."

"There's a little more," Mark murmured. "Roger West told me what happened last evening, and who was here with you— hold it!" he exclaimed as Harrington began to scowl, and to open his mouth. "I'm not interested in your private affairs. Nor is West. You might pay some attention to us, though. You're moving towards as tight a corner as you've ever known. Bellowing about like an angry bull won't make the police think more kindly of you. I suppose you realize what you *are* doing," he added, proffering his case.

Harrington brushed it aside.

"If the police are still taking heed of what that raddled old buzzard said, God help them. Apart from that, I'm not aware that anything has been said or done which affects me. I had the misfortune to be born a cousin to Claude Prendergast."

"Misfortune is nearer the mark than you know," said Mark. "Someone killed the other Prendergasts, and had a shot at Claude. If Claude dies, you inherit."

"Do you want me to buy Claude a life-belt," demanded Harrington. "Well, do you?"

Mark smiled. "Not quite that, he isn't likely to die just yet, he's being too closely watched. But there are deeper waters. You haven't given anyone else any credit yet, you know. Last night another director of *Dreem* was killed, and last night also a man attempted to do bodily harm to a certain Gabriel Potter. Now I dislike Potter as much as anyone could, but I don't think the right way to stop his dirty game is to bump him off. It's careless, it's messy, and even if he'd committed a dozen murders, which isn't by any means certain, murdering him earns the gallows."

Harrington eyed Mark stonily.

"And why are you reading this riot act?"

"Don't you know?"

"For Pete's sake!" exclaimed Harrington, "I'm too tired to start following your verbal circles. No, I don't."

Mark said: "What does the name David Anderson mean to you?"

He saw Harrington start, and felt that he had scored a hit. Then he grew less sure. The name was familiar enough, but to

Mark it appeared that Harrington was far more puzzled than worried as he said with deep feeling:

"If he comes near me inside the next twenty-four hours, I'll fire him, and never mind what the Government says. The little twerp was due on duty last night, but didn't turn up. A trimming machine went wrong, and I've spent all night putting it right. If he'd had any conscience he wouldn't have left the thing in such a condition. A breakdown was inevitable." Harrington drew a deep breath, and then went on to give his further opinion of David Anderson. The man had remained in Harrington's employ because of his engineering ability, and something else, which wasn't clear.

Harrington ran out of words. Mark, standing and watching the man, felt a restraint in him. Although Harrington let himself go up to a point, there was nothing vindictive in his manner. Anderson had let him down, and not for the first time. Throughout the harangue Mark perceived in Harrington a consciousness of what could be done, and what was beyond the pale. Harrington did not actually put it into words, but he implied that Anderson owed it to his country not to slack—but he slacked a great deal.

Harrington gave a sudden, almost boyish grin.

"For some odd reason, that's made me feel better! But that's no reason why you should grin like a cheetah. I'm going to lock those le Fleur pieces up, you don't look honest." He paused. "What has Anderson got to do with you, anyhow?"

"He's the man who attempted bodily harm on Potter," said Mark, sweetly.

"*What!*"

Mark ran a hand tenderly over his head, and said:

"Y'know, Harrington, you're either a clever beggar or you're too damned ingenuous. *What!* indeed. You heard me: Anderson tried to kill or injure Potter." He saw disbelief dawn in Harrington's eyes, and something else; it might have been horror, or dread, or sheer stupefaction—and it might have been that Harrington was just tired out.

"I don't believe it," Harrington said flatly.

"The police will convince you, and I don't mean Roger West. Did Anderson have a motor-cycle?"

"Yes."

"He reached it. I stopped him, and someone was foolish enough to shoot him. Dead," added Mark. "It was a quick end for him, but will mean a lot of questions. You see, he attacked Potter at Transom's house. Near Transom's house McFallen was killed last night, also. The Transom *ménage* is coming in for a lot of inspection, and the Transom and Anderson connection with you makes it peculiar. Don't you think so?"

Harrington backed heavily to a chair.

"It's the most incredible story I've ever heard," he said. "I'm still inclined not to believe it." He was not at all convincing. He stretched out a hand. "Give me a cigarette, will you? . . . thanks." He accepted a light, and added slowly: "I knew nothing about this. I can't fathom it—I can't see the connection. Anderson was nothing to do with me outside work, he wasn't even a personal friend. As a matter of fact, I detested him. He was never reliable and he was always lying to get time off, or threatening to find another job if he didn't get this indulgence or that. He was so clever at his job that he had me in a cleft stick."

"What was his job?" demanded Mark.

Harrington frowned. "I don't see that it's your business and I don't see that it matters much, anyhow. He was a machine specialist in the one part, and a rubber chemist in the other. He combined both jobs, and was just the man I needed. He—" Harrington drew in too much smoke and coughed. "He's going to take some replacing."

"I wish that I knew a little more," said Mark broodingly. "Are rubber chemists so rare?"

"When they've got the ingenuity that he had, yes. You can ask as much as you like, but his job remains my secret."

"Why are you so secretive?"

"In the first place, because I'm sworn to it. In the second, because it happens to be my business. I can't see where the Transoms are concerned with Anderson," he added.

"Do you know them well?"

"By reputation, but I haven't met the family. They wouldn't approve of me." There was a twist to his grin as he stood up. "So I'm to expect questions from the police about Anderson, am I? Potter was attacked by him, and—it just doesn't make sense!"

"Couldn't you help it to?" asked Mark.

"No," said Harrington firmly. He then looked past Mark towards the door. "No," he repeated slowly. "I don't believe even Anderson would do anything like that."

There was a faraway look in his eyes, an expression which could not be mistaken; it was fear. Not necessarily personal fear, but probably of something which he could see and which would be disastrous, which he could not avoid. Mark imagined all that while Harrington stared past him.

Harrington said abruptly:

"Do the police know you've come here?"

"No."

"Not even West?"

"Not even West. I wanted to see how you took all this."

Harrington shrugged.

"Thanks for coming." He hesitated, then went on with a twisted smile: "I'm egoistical enough to think you came to give me a warning, thinking one was necessary. It wasn't, but thanks all the same. I've no idea why Anderson had a down on Potter. All I know about Anderson is what I've told you, added to the fact that he's been pretty flush with money lately. I thought he had been backing winners, he did a lot of betting. Now, if you don't mind, I'm going to get some rest. I'm in no condition to be interrogated by the police yet. I don't want to fly off the handle again," he added slowly, "but West got me on the raw last night. I thought he'd been following my—fiancée."

"You didn't give him any encouragement to think you were going to help in any way."

"He'll get over it," said Harrington. He stifled a yawn. "I'm not going to talk to you any more."

Mark left the flat.

The call had been inconclusive, yet he could not hide a feeling that Harrington had kept some vital piece of information back. The mystery of Harrington and his small factory loomed larger in Mark's mind, but as he went slowly back to Chelsea he wondered whether he was not trying to follow too many trails.

He dwelt on Potter.

He did not doubt that Potter had persuaded the trio at Yew House not to protest to the police about his presence there. He fancied that he knew why; Potter would imagine that he thus had some kind of a lever to use against him. Mark smiled, wondering why Potter had wanted him to go to his office. He wished that the arrangement had not been cancelled.

But he could not get his mind off Harrington and Garielle Transom. They obsessed him.

He made himself some tea at his flat, munched a biscuit, and wondered what to do next.

He walked slowly to Roger's office, hoped there were not too many people in it, and on entering saw the head and shoulders of a girl in RAF blue above the back of a chair opposite Roger. Mark exclaimed enough to make the girl look round sharply. It was Garielle Transom.

13

EXCHANGE OF IDEAS

Roger hardly knew whether to be pleased or sorry as he stood up and smiled. He had got the other DIs out of the room, succeeding with Eddie Day only when Eddie Day had been called to a Superintendent's office.

"Miss Transom, this is Mr. Mark Lessing," he said. "Mark, I don't think you've met Miss Transom."

"My bad luck," said Mark, and won a smile. He took a chair at one end of the desk, at Roger's wave of the hand. Roger went on:

"Mr. Lessing has been giving me some assistance in the case, Miss Transom. I hope that you don't mind if he sits in."

"I didn't come to object to anything," said Garielle. "As I've told you, Inspector, I came to try to explain why Mr. Harrington was so upset last evening."

Mark half-closed his eyes, and listened. Roger could form the necessary conclusions. Not that Garielle Transom had a lot to say; Harrington had been overworking lately and his work was of considerable importance; he was troubled because so many people had recently shown an interest in him. Also, there was a dislike, tantamount to prejudice, which Harrington felt for all the directors of *Dreem*—her father included. She did not try to explain that prejudice, just offered it as a fact.

Mark opened his eyes.

Roger was leaning back in his chair with a wry expression on his face.

"Miss Transom, why *did* you come to see me?"

Garielle's only reaction was to sit up more straightly in her chair, and say abruptly:

"I want to know why you are interested in Mr. Harrington, Inspector."

"Because he is a cousin of Claude Prendergast," said Roger. "I don't need to tell you of the Prendergast misadventures."

"Does that really answer my question?"

"Yes. It's our only reason. We hoped Mr. Harrington could give us more information. If there is any information that you can give us we shall be equally grateful."

"And if there isn't, will I please go?" Garielle smiled but did not look wholly at ease. She fidgeted with a glove in her lap. The silence lengthened, neither man making any attempt to fill the gap. Finally she spoke in a crisper voice; it was easy to imagine she had reached some kind of a decision.

"I thought you might like to know that Mr. Harrington and I met quite by accident, and that we were on very friendly terms before he realized that I was Arthur Transom's daughter. I have already tried to explain his mood last evening, but—I am not sure that I know the full explanation. Will you please answer this? Do you think there is any danger for him?"

Roger shrugged.

"I can't say yes and I can't say no. We have to keep all possibilities in mind, and that's obviously one of them. If you want to know whether I have had any positive indication of danger for Mr. Harrington, the answer is 'no.'" He paused, but saw no relief in her eyes. He was puzzled. "Have you?"

"No," replied Garielle. "But I wish I knew why he was quite so worried. He *is*, you know. You must have seen that."

"It looked rather like it, but it's difficult to judge on brief acquaintance. How long has he seemed worried?"

"For six months or so."

"From about the time of Septimus Prendergast's death," remarked Roger.

"I suppose that coincidence is too obvious to be missed." Garielle was making a little ball of her glove. "Yes, it would be about that time, but I don't think there's any reason for believing that they're connected—Bill's worry and the deaths, I mean. He's not interested in the *Dreem* people. In fact he dislikes them utterly, he—" she drew a deep breath, and added: "He has definite ideas about profit and profit motives, and he thinks that far too much is made out of tobacco."

"Do you?" Mark murmured the question, hardly expecting an answer and glancing at Roger for forgiveness.

Garielle looked at him.

"No more than in many forms of industry. But I'm not interested in *Dreem*, Mr. Lessing, my differences with my family have been on very personal grounds." She smiled, as if to point out to Mark that he could not put leading questions without it being observed, then stopped rolling her gloves, pulling one on quickly and pushing methodically down between the fingers. "I must be going. I've taken too much of your time already. Inspector, can I rely on you to do everything possible to make sure that my fiancé is quite safe?"

"Yes. But I wish you would give me more idea why you're afraid that he's not."

"I can't, it's just premonition. Don't laugh too much at feminine intuition, will you? And thank you for being so patient." She was about to push her chair back when Mark drew it back for her. Together they saw her to the door. She walked like a dream.

When she had gone, Mark said:

"There goes my idea of beauty, *per se*. Harrington is a luckier man than he knows. I wonder how long they've been engaged— even whether in fact they are engaged?"

"We'll find out," said Roger.

"I hope you aren't going to have to wash a lot of dirty linen for that girl," Mark said. "How long had she been here before I turned up?"

"You heard all that mattered," Roger told him. "What did you make of it?"

"What could I make? She's worried about Harrington, she isn't sure how deeply he's involved, she wanted to emphasise that he's not on good terms with her family and the *Dreem* mob *in toto*, but she went a shade too far. She tried to say that his objection to the *Dreem* directors is founded on an altruistic and moral motive, but of course there's something much deeper. Also she lied, I think." He paused, and added: "Apart from the attempts to get us thinking on the wrong lines, she lied at least once."

"On the matter of their meeting accidentally?"

"There are limits to coincidences."

"It could have been one," said Roger. "We can't rule it out. When we know the whole story I may fit it in, but I'd like to know what really prompted her to come. She surely didn't think I'd talk." He tapped a cigarette against his thumbnail, while through the open window there boomed the chiming of Big Ben. "It's a quarter past one. Let's get out for some lunch, and you can tell me where you've been hiding yourself."

"I was a victim of a chapter of accidents," declared Mark, as Roger picked up his hat. "What do you make of the latest Delaware village murder?"

"McFallen? I haven't heard anything fresh."

"No, not McFallen. The unknown gentleman."

Roger shot him a sideways glance.

"I haven't heard of any."

Mark stopped in the middle of a stride, recovered quickly, and did not speak for some seconds. Then he commented on the oddness of the fact that Lampard had been so secretive.

They were in the hall when a sergeant came hurrying towards them, calling Roger. In his hand he held a sealed envelope, and on his face there was an expression suggesting that he had a great weight on his mind.

"This letter came for you from Guildford, early this morning, sir. It was delivered by hand." He gulped the words.

Roger said: "How early?"

"It arrived just about nine o'clock, sir."

"Then why haven't I had it before?"

The sergeant gulped again. "It was filed in the wrong basket, sir, and went out to one of the Divisions. It's just been returned. My fault, sir. I was superintending the post this morning."

"Oh, all right." Roger turned back to the office with Mark.

It was a long and detailed report of the murder near Yew House, including a statement signed by Potter, Transom, Widdison, and Hauteby. There was a note that Mark had confirmed the general accuracy. There were photographs of the dead man, and a request for Yard assistance to get him identified.

"That bloody sergeant!" exclaimed Roger bitterly. "I—but now Mark, what do you know about this?"

"I can give you some help, and you won't need to worry about the identity of the gent. I knew last night but kept it to myself so as to try to work more effectively on Harrington."

He plunged into his story, which filled in many details missing from Lampard's report, and only once did Roger interrupt, to say:

"Harrington didn't like Anderson?"

"No," agreed Mark. "But I don't know whether that's anything to go on. Harrington was at the factory all night, remember."

"You were told that by someone on the telephone, but he might have arrived at the factory any time during the night."

Roger pressed a bell.

Sergeant Sloane, large, self-effacing, somewhat elephantine in size and movement, entered promptly.

"Sloane, try to check up whether Mr. William Harrington was

working in his factory last night," Roger said, "and if so what time he arrived and what time he left. The factory is—"

"I know the address, sir, thank you," said Sloane, and effaced himself.

Roger pulled the telephone near and called Guildford. Lampard was at lunch, but Inspector Wade was in his office. Roger reported what he knew about the identity of the dead man.

"Yes, Mr. West, I know. We've just discovered some papers that identify him. They were lying in a ditch near where he was found. I have a report ready for Mr. Lampard as soon as he gets back from lunch."

"Good. Tell him that I am going to see Anderson's employer."

He rang off, tipped his hat to the back of his head, and looked sardonically at Mark.

"So the identification papers were found in a ditch, were they? I wonder what little bird put them there? Come on, let's feed."

"It's my turn to pay," said Mark in subdued tones.

"I'll say it's your turn!" Roger went silent, and kept it up until they were having a glass of beer at a *brasserie* in Cannon Row. Then Roger said:

"Harrington dislikes the Prendergasts, and look what happens to them. Harrington dislikes Anderson, and—"

"I looked at what happened to him," admitted Mark. "But I don't believe Harrington was responsible for it."

"I hope not," Roger said moodily. "But circumstantial evidence is piling up against him, you know. I wonder if he's much of a shot?"

"Globe-trotters often are," said Mark.

They continued to exchange views, impressions, and ideas freely.

Presently Roger said:

"We thought that Potter looked after Abie, but did Potter look after Anderson? Was it a fake to make it look as if Potter was attacked, or was it genuine? If so, what reason had Anderson for disliking Potter to that extent?"

"If that was a fake, I wasn't there," said Mark. "Potter didn't lose his head, as Transom did. He moved pretty fast, and he wasn't waiting for the trouble. If I hadn't cried out there would have been a nasty hole on Potter's head, and I don't mean maybe. I think," Mark added abruptly, "that I'll go to see Morgan."

Roger glanced at his watch.

"Yes, it's half-past two. I must get back, Janet should be home soon, but she'll be all right. Why do you want to see Morgan?"

"He mentioned some unknowns who visited Potter," Mark said.

He reached Morgan's office half an hour later, entered after a tap, and saw Pep sitting on the corner of the typist's desk swinging his brightly polished shoes. He was dictating at speed, and held up a hand to Mark for silence while he finished.

"Get that done as soon as you can. They want to use it in court in the morning, and the learned counsel needs a few hours with it before he starts talking." He showed his teeth in a beaming smile to Mark. "Hallo, Mr. Lessing, how are you this morning?"

"Good afternoon," said Mark, as he was led into the smaller office.

"So it is," agreed Morgan. "Now Mr. Lessing, I don't want to know a thing about what happened after I'd gone last night. Not a thing, please. We're in deep waters as it is, and I don't even like getting my feet wet." His beam widened. "What can I do for you now?"

"How soon can you get at your man, the one who's watching Potter's office?" asked Mark. "I want to find whether he can identify this chap." He took a photograph of Anderson from his pocket.

Morgan squinted down, then rounded his desk to pull open a deep drawer and extract a manila file. From it he took several small photographs, and handed them to Mark.

"My man took snaps with a Leica," he reported. "Your man

was there, Mr. Lessing *and* others. Look at them—just look at them!"

Mark held the snaps, stared down, and went very still.

There were several faces which he did not recognize, but the two that fascinated him were those of Anderson and Garielle Transom—both visitors to Gabriel Potter on the previous morning.

"A surprise, eh?" asked Morgan. "I thought it might be. I had a look round Kingston yesterday, and discovered the little lady visiting Harrington. Then I had her photograph checked. I found out who she was. That's why I told you to go and see Harrington," added Morgan. "I'd been told she was there all night and I thought you might catch 'em both. Peculiar situation, Mr. Lessing, isn't it?"

"Yes, Pep, peculiar's the word." Mark eyed Morgan very thoughtfully. "You wouldn't know whether Harrington is much use with a rifle, would you?"

"First-class shot!" said Morgan promptly. "Learned that from one of his workmen. Harrington's in the Home Guard, and gets on the possible every time they have target practice. Tell you another thing, Mr. Lessing. Transom can't shoot for nuts, and nor can Potter, but Widdison and Hauteby are dead-shots. Both Bisley marksmen. I checked it this morning, I'd knew you'd want to know sooner or later."

14

HARRINGTON TALKS

Mark left Morgan's office at half-past three, and walked briskly down the Strand. He slackened his pace as he neared Potter's building, hesitated, and went in. The lift was working.

In Potter's outer office the massive bodyguard was standing by a desk, licking stamps.

"Hallo, George," said Mark genially. "Is the man of the law in?"

"Supposing he is?"

"Thank you," said Mark, and pushed up the flap of the counter leading to Potter's private office. George dropped his stamps and barred the way. A diminutive creature by a small private switchboard plugged in to Potter, and asked:

"Can you see Mr. Lessing, please?" She paused, pulled out the plug, and said, like a child repeating a lesson: "Mr. Potter will see Mr. Lessing, George."

George glowered as if that were a personal affront, but removed himself from Mark's path. Mark made a rat-tat-tat on the glass panel of the door, and entered the long, musty office, beaming at Potter's expressionless face. Potter was putting papers into the pigeon-holes of the big roll-top desk.

"I thought I'd come after all," Mark said.

"I am not surprised at your visit," said Potter. "Sit down, Mr. Lessing, I would like to talk to you."

Mark deposited his hat, stick, and gloves, and sat down.

"That's nice to know."

"You will be wise to listen attentively," said Potter. "You may make many foolish mistakes if you don't." He pushed his chair back and rested a thin, scraggy hand on a sealed envelope in front of him. "In there is a full statement of what really happened last night. Your friend Inspector West would not be able to ignore the statement of how you forced entry, if it were sent to him in his official capacity."

Mark put his head to one side.

"No, I suppose not," he said. "Except that it can't be an accurate statement, as you don't know how I got there. Between you and me, I'm not going to be frightened. That weapon has two edges, and you'll cut yourself if you're not careful. For instance, you lied. Lampard wouldn't like that. Transom also lied."

Potter said: "Transom encouraged the police to believe you had some right there. I did not. I discovered the real truth afterwards. My written statement makes that quite clear."

"A double-cross on Transom, is it? That means you don't like Transom, all of a sudden."

"My regard for Transom does not come into the matter," said Potter. "Mr. Lessing, I have been hoping to see you in order to warn you very seriously. You are most ill-advised to continue your inquiries. The Inspector cannot help himself, but there is no reason why you should put yourself in danger. I speak as a friend," Potter went on, glibly. "I should be grieved to hear that anything had happened to you."

"Oh?" said Mark. "How long have we been friends?"

Potter leaned forward and placed a hand on Mark's knee. Even through his trousers Mark felt the coldness of the touch, but he was far more startled by Potter's words.

"Since your shout of warning last night, Mr. Lessing."

"No!"

"You can be facetious if you wish. I believe that I owe you my life. I am not a man likely to be unmindful of such a debt. I can tell you nothing, but I can warn you. You are in no danger from me, but then you would never have thought that likely." He did not smile, but went on flatly: "There is danger to me, Mr. Lessing, and to you. In fact, there is danger to everyone who interests themselves in the affairs of the *Dreem* company. I was invited to assist the directors legally. I believe that you heard me refusing, last night. I shall continue to do my best for my clients, Mr. and Mrs. Prendergast, but I have seen enough of the activities in and about Delaware village to feel that it would not be wise for me to take any deeper interest. If it is not wise for me, Mr. Lessing, it is certainly most hazardous for you."

After a startled pause, Mark said:

"Well I'm damned!"

"An incident which meant the saving of my life may be inconsequential to you," said Potter. "To me it is of considerable importance. Mr. Lessing—will any consideration in money or in kind persuade you to relax your efforts?"

Mark swallowed hard.

"If it will," said Potter, "I may be able to arrange one substantial enough to have the desired effect."

Mark swallowed again, and took out a cigarette. He was more surprised than he had ever been, as much by Potter's expression of real sincerity as by the offered bribe.

Potter leaned forward with a match.

"Thank you," said Mark, and drew hard. "Potter, I might have been deceived in you after all. I didn't think you had a single shred of decency in your make-up. However, it's no dice. You didn't expect it to be a deal. But—couldn't we reach other terms?"

"There is nothing else I have to discuss with you," said Potter.

Mark stood up, paused, and as Potter said nothing, left the office. He nodded to George without making a quip, and let the office door slam behind him. He approached the lift slowly. It was waiting on the fifth floor, with its iron doors closed. He opened them, and was about to step inside when the lift began to drop.

He saw the lift floor disappearing beneath him as he stepped towards it, and flung himself backwards. His stick caught between the top of the lift and the main floor, and snapped into several pieces. His hat was crushed, and he thudded against the wall heavily, jolting himself painfully. The lift continued to fall, until it crashed to the bottom. The crash shook the iron-walled lift-well, the map of Old London, the windows, the doors. It brought people shouting and exclaiming, made doors open all along the passages, and all down the centre of the building.

Mark straightened up, dazed. The handle of his stick, with its silver top, remained in his hand. His wrist was painful where it had been jarred when the stick had caught.

George came rushing out of Potter's office.

Mark stared at him, less dazedly, as George said in a hoarse voice:

"Are you all right? That damned lift . . ."

Mark pushed past him, reaching Potter's outer office and ignoring the typists and the girl at the switchboard. He saw her push in a plug, but before she could call Potter he had pushed open the door of the inner office. Potter looked up from his desk, and for the first time Mark saw fear on the man's drab face.

Potter pushed his chair back.

"Lessing! What are you—"

Mark said nothing. His face was livid, his eyes were burning. He took two steps forward, gripped Potter's shoulder, and pulled him nearer. He bunched his right hand and drove it on to Potter's chin. He heard the *crack!* of the blow, and saw Potter's eyes roll. The man would have fallen had Mark not continued to hold him.

From the door, a girl screamed.

Mark let Potter go. The man crumpled up, and sprawled over his desk. Mark turned. The girl jumped to one side. George was entering the outer office, but at sight of Mark's expression he stood still. Mark passed him blindly, then went out, down the stairs and into the coolness of the street.

It was a welcome coolness. He breathed deeply. He looked at his watch, cursed the fact that he could not buy a drink, but went into the nearest café for some tea.

He felt very much better twenty minutes later, and took a taxi to the Yard.

. . . .

"What's made you so mad?" Roger asked him.

Mark told him everything.

"D'you think Potter would have stopped the lift trick if you'd come to terms?" Roger asked.

"Probably," said Mark. "I think he meant what he said. But why the hell pull that one so soon afterwards? What do I know, Roger? Damn it, even Potter wouldn't rig that booby-trap for me unless it really mattered. I've stumbled on something gargantuan in size, heaven knows what."

Roger drew at his cigarette.

"So Garielle Transom and David Anderson visited Potter yesterday morning. They weren't together, were they?"

"Pep didn't say so. He would have done."

"Yes. What do you think we should do next?"

"The same as you, I hope."

"Harrington," murmured Roger. "Another, much more positive interview with Mr. William Harrington. It's time he stopped being so secretive. I had another idea after we split up," he added, "and got Sloane busy again with the Ministry of Supply. Harrington's factory is controlled by them, and I want to know what he's doing. I told Sloane to ring me at Harrington's flat at half-past five, if I hadn't countermanded the order. Just in case of accidents I've asked Lampard of Guildford to keep an eye on Harrington's place."

"Odd thing," said Mark. "I asked Pep Morgan to do the same thing. Any objection if I come?"

"We can do this together. It's going to be strictly legal, but you'll add the touch of informality Harrison may like. Oh, while

I remember—" he opened his wallet and extracted some pink petrol coupons. "There's twelve gallons, but go easy with them. I had to perjure myself to get 'em."

"Heartfelt thanks," said Mark. "I'll tell you what, let's go in my car."

"Mine's nearer," said Roger.

He drove at speed to Kingston, explaining that he had learned about Harrington's prowess with a rifle, and the shooting ability of the *Dreem* directors. He hoped he wouldn't have to wait long, or go to the factory.

He need not have worried, for Harrington opened the door. He was wearing a blue dressing-gown over his shirt and trousers. His welcome was not enthusiastic.

"You again?" he said. "And both together. You'll have to be bloody careful."

Roger said: "When are you going to stop being bloody-minded?" He stepped into the box of a hall, and was led into the lounge-cum-dining-room. Harrington eyed him warily, and said:

"I've been waiting for you."

"That's better than trying to dodge me. Where were you last night?"

"At my factory. Didn't *he* tell you?"

"What time did you go there?"

"About half-past ten."

"Did you stay in the factory all night?"

"I was there until after seven this morning."

"Can you give me the names of any people who saw you?"

"Twenty or thirty, if you'll come over to the factory with me." Harrington began to fill his pipe. "I didn't shoot Anderson, if that's what you're driving at. I've often felt like it, but I didn't."

"I hope not," said Roger grimly. "Did you know that Anderson was acquainted with Potter?"

Harrington stopped work on the pipe.

"I certainly did not."

"How long have you known Potter?"

"I've told you, and I'm not wasting my time going over it again."

"You'd never met him before?"

"No."

"He's never approached you on any matter except that which you have told me about?"

"The grammar's bad but the context is right," said Harrington. "No, he hasn't."

"Does the same apply to Mrs. Prendergast?"

"It does."

"Claude Prendergast?"

"Yes," said Harrington and turned away to get some matches from the mantelpiece.

"Had you ever known the other Prendergasts?"

"They weren't people I wanted to know."

"That's not answering the question," Roger snapped. "Harrington, I'm going to have the whole truth from you. If you won't give it me here, we'll go to the Yard. Had you ever known the Prendergasts?"

Harrington eyed the bowl of his pipe, then looked at Roger squarely, and said:

"Yes."

"What were the circumstances?"

Harrington drew a deep breath.

"I knew they were wealthy, and was foolish enough to think they would be interested in financing a small venture. I wanted their backing, I had something which I believed would one day make a fortune. In spite of their moral obligations, they refused."

"All of them?"

"Yes."

"Did anyone else know of the proposition?"

Harrington hesitated. He looked massive and tough, but Mark had an idea that he was relieved by the trend of the questions.

"Yes, they did," he said at last. "All the *Dreem* directors knew of it. That—" he paused—"was how I met Miss Transom. There was an informal meeting of the *Dreem* company board, and she had driven her father over from Yew House. That was just after the outbreak of war," Harrington went on, "and I had newly arrived in England. I felt sore about being turned down, and approached Transom privately. He also turned me down, and we had a few words—he can be a rude devil. I was feeling very raw. If you'd like the more intimate details," Harrington went on, "Garielle later had a row with her family about it. That's why she joined the WAAFs when she did. The primary cause of her row," Harrington went on, "was that she continued to see me, although her father 'forbade' it. When Potter got in touch with me, I thought it might be because the firm had changed its mind, and wanted to put money into my business. Believe me, I longed for them to make the offer, so that I could turn it down. I've been wanting a chance to do that ever since the first negotiations."

"So you've got enough financial backing now?" asked Roger.

"Doesn't it look like it?"

"Who financed you?"

"I don't see that it affects the case," said Harrington. "I was asked not to disclose his name."

Roger said grimly: "He didn't expect the police to be interested."

"I'll pass him your question," Harrington said easily.

It was then, just when they appeared to be at an *impasse*, that the telephone rang. It was just within Harrington's reach, and he stretched forward, lifted the receiver, and then said in obvious surprise:

"Yes, hold on." He looked up at Roger. "It's for you."

"Thanks." Roger took the receiver and heard the flat voice of Sergeant Sloane.

"Reporting as requested, sir," said Sloane. "I've been able to check on all the matters you left with me. The gentleman was at his factory from ten o'clock last night until seven o'clock this morning. He was observed by at least twenty people all the time, as he worked on a machine which had broken down and held up production for one of the departments."

"Good," said Roger.

"The Company in question is concerned with the manufacturing of rubber parts for aero-engines, tanks, and naval craft," went on Sloane, as if reading from his report. "Its Research Department, called the Development Department, is engaged on exploratory work in connection with synthetic rubber. The Ministry of Supply particularly requests that no hint of this is given to the Press, sir."

"Oh," said Roger. "I get it. Anything else?"

"Not at the moment, sir."

"Thanks." Roger rang off. Staring at Harrington, he was faced for the first time with the fact that Harrington was probably one of the few men in the country fully equipped for investigating the processes for the manufacture of synthetic rubber. It was a development vital to the national interest at a time when the natural rubber sources in Malaya and much of the Dutch East Indies were in the hands of the Japanese. And it was just as important to the future economic soundness of the nation.

15

ANYTHING MORE?

Roger sat down again, glanced at Mark and back at Harrington before saying heavily:

"Have you any specific objection to Mr. Lessing knowing what you're working on? I've just had a confidential report, but I'm prepared to tell him."

"That's your pigeon," Harrington said. "So you've got it as quickly as that," he added ruminatively. "I suppose it was inevitable. I'm working on synthetic rubber, the first to be simple and cheap to manufacture. I've had special machinery installed at Dean Park. Anderson was one of the few men who really knew what he was doing in the experimental stage. My company," went on Harrington with deep satisfaction, "is going to expand tenfold. I've a big new factory almost ready, and it will be large enough to cope with twenty-five per cent of British rubber requirements once it's in operation. I'm already out of the experimental stage."

Mark broke his silence.

"We see a genius before us," he said solemnly.

"This isn't funny," said Harrington. "I've spent a lot of time in the Far East, and if you'd seen the slow way we get rubber and cure it, you'd know that with increasing consumption we need new and revolutionary sources of supply. I started off trying to find a better way of curing crude rubber, then went on to one development after another. Once the war started, it was all Singapore to an onion that there would be trouble with the Japs, and that they'd go straight for the rubber and the oil. I came here and set to work on a synthetic product. Naturally I haven't wanted the fact known too widely. Nor has the Ministry of Supply."

"Did all the *Dreem* people know of this?" Roger asked.

"They knew I was making synthetic rubber. I don't think they knew anything else. Why?"

"He means that we've been searching for a motive for the murder of the Prendergasts," said Mark. "We'd concentrated on *Dreem* cigarettes and the Company. It could be nothing to do with *Dreem*, but only with you. What's the estimated value of your process?"

Harrington gave a bark of a laugh.

"I couldn't give a value. When it's fully exploited it will make the *Dreem* company look small. It's outsize. You don't need me to tell you that. And it's simple enough, while there's nothing very difficult about raw materials. It's partly from coal, partly from certain ores and oils."

"And Anderson knew the process?"

"Yes, he did."

"When you said last night that 'it couldn't be anything like that,'" said Mark, "you meant that it had occurred to you that Anderson might have been selling the secret process?"

"I did. It would be foul if he had."

Roger put in: "Anderson might have sold out to Potter, and been double-crossed. That could explain why he had a go at Gabby, and why he was killed. All roads lead to Potter. I'll find what they've been doing between 'em," he added. "May I use your phone?" He was soon connected with Sloane. "About the dead man Anderson," he said quickly. "Concentrate on his association with Gabriel Potter, will you? Get a full story as quickly as you can."

"Right you are, sir."

Roger replaced the receiver.

"Just for the record, Mr. Harrington, I would like to see your passport, and the other documents of identification." He did not smile, but his eyes were amused. "Mrs. Claude Prendergast apart, I need to see them."

"Please yourself," said Harrington. "They're in my bureau. I've a box-room I use as a study-cum-lab. Would you like to see me take them out of the drawer?"

"We'll trust you," said Roger amiably.

Harrington nodded. He went out. Quite suddenly Mark got up, opened the piano, and began to play very gently.

He conjured magic out of the keys, yet Roger felt irritated; he did not want music or anything else to interfere with his thoughts, already varied enough, but he found himself listening against his will. He did not notice Harrington return and stand in the doorway, watching Mark. It was an odd interlude, made more unreal when Mark stopped and swung about on the stool.

"Forgive the liberty," he said.

Roger turned to look at Harrington, and as he did so, saw a shadowy movement at one side of the man. He shouted: "Look out!" and leapt forward.

Harrington swung round.

Now Roger saw the shadow materialize into a man's hand and arm. The man held a length of iron bar. It rose and fell, catching Harrington on the side of the head. Harrington fell sideways.

Roger rushed forward. The man who entered came at a run, taking a flying kick at his hand. Roger snatched his hand away.

Mark, just behind him, drew in a sharp breath.

Behind the first man was a second, smaller one. He held a gun, and covered both Mark and Roger. Roger had a quick vision of flame, a stab of imaginary pain, as if a bullet had entered his chest.

"Get back, the two of you," the gunman ordered.

The big man put a hand to Mark's pocket and drew out an automatic. He grinned.

"Think you're clever, don't you?"

"Clay, put that gun away," Roger made himself say. "You must be crazy."

"You're the crazy one," said Charlie Clay. He stood, large and hulking, rather undecided, as if he did not know what to do next. The smaller man joined him. They stood in the doorway, each holding a gun.

"Turn around," ordered Clay.

"If you don't do what I say—" Roger began.

Clay moved forward, jerking his gun up.

Roger saw the ugly face and the bunched hand—the big ugly hand so dextrous at opening safes.

"Turn around," he said harshly. "I won't say it again."

The little gunman put his gun back in his pocket. He took out something else: two long, silk scarves. He bent down and wound one about Harrington's face, then as Mark turned he looped the second about his head, knotted it, and drew it tight. It was all done with great precision, and Mark made no attempt to struggle.

Roger said in a stony voice:

"So you tied the towel round him before, did you?"

"Shut up," said Clay.

He watched Roger closely, while the little man tied Mark's wrists behind his back, then did the same to Harrington's, with pieces of tape. Roger thought: they should be easy to break. Then almost before he realized that the man was ready for him, another scarf dropped over his face, was drawn tightly back and knotted. He knew then why Mark had been so helpless. The sudden tightening made him choke. He drew an inward breath and could not breathe out properly. He was heaving for breath when his hands were jerked behind him, and tied. He could see above the scarf. He forced himself not to struggle, knowing that would make his breathing even more difficult.

Clay jerked Roger round towards the door. In the hall he turned him towards another door, one which Roger had not yet seen open. It was a box-room. Roger could see a bench along one wall, a dozen or more instruments on it, bottles, glasses, what looked like a square steel box, a bunsen burner, and a small machine, almost a miniature, in one corner. Against the other wall was a bureau, next to it a filing cabinet. There was room for only one chair, between the bureau and the bench. The walls were lined to the ceiling with shelves, crowded with bottles; it was a small laboratory, well-equipped.

Clay pushed him violently.

Roger had no control over himself, and fell heavily to the floor. The sudden effort to breathe made it impossible for him to think of anything else. He was still on the floor when Mark was brought in and pushed over in exactly the same way. They were struggling to get to sitting positions when Harrington was carried in and dropped beside them.

With the three men here, there was only just room for the door to close.

Clay said something; it sounded like "bloody dicks." He took a can from the bench, opened it, and began to pour its liquid contents on to the bureau. It splashed over Harrington's body and Mark's legs; the stench of oil was so strong it made them catch their breath.

Roger heaved as he thought: "My God, *petrol*."

Through the fringe of the scarf he could see Clay's vague face. The little eyes were glittering. He dropped the tin with a clatter. It struck Roger's ankle, but he was hardly aware of the sharp pain.

"Be careful," the other man muttered.

"Get outside," ordered Charlie Clay. He took a box of matches from his pocket. As Roger saw it, a dozen thoughts flashed through his mind. He felt less afraid than bereft of ordinary feeling, his mind working quite dispassionately.

Petrol was used for treating rubber, the fire could easily appear accidental. The tape and the scarves about their faces would burn swiftly, their flimsiness was now explained; they would leave no trace. There was no window in the box-room, smoke would not be seen until there was a fierce conflagration; it would be far too late to bring help.

The thing that his mind boggled at was Clay's part in this. Clay was a cracksman, Clay—

The big man drew a match along the box. The head fell off; there was a single spark, but nothing else.

Clay was standing in the doorway; the other man hidden behind him. Obviously they were afraid of an explosion, of getting hurt if a blast of flame shot up once the match was dropped.

Before he tried again, Clay started; and Roger heard the sound at the same time, feeling his heart thump wildly.

There was a loud knock on the front door.

. . . .

Clay disappeared from the room.

Roger's mouth and nose were filled with the petrol fumes and his heart would not stop thumping. He tried to move, but his cramped position made it difficult and he could only stare towards the door. A mutter of voices followed, as if Clay and his companion were having an argument.

The knock was repeated.

Roger heard the footsteps going along the hall. He imagined that the little man went to the door, and heard it open. A voice travelled to him, but he could not recognize it. There was a louder voice, a shout, and the door banged.

Then heavy, thudding footsteps.

The door swung open, banged against Harrington's foot, and swung back on Clay, who had appeared for a split second with a bunch of matches in one hand and the box in the other. Matches and box fell, and Clay gasped as the door struck him on the face. The other man was shouting:

"Come on, come on!"

Footsteps again, and then a fresh thundering on the front door, the opening of others. A different sound, which Roger imagined was that of Clay and his companion going down the iron fire-escape.

The only thing certain was that they were on the run.

The thundering on the front door increased, and then was replaced by a different sound, as of splintering wood. But there was a long wait before the man who forced an entry reached the box-room. He pushed cautiously against the door, and then looked round it.

Roger gasped incoherently:

"Lampard!"

Behind the Guildford man was Pep Morgan. Morgan's bright teeth showed not in a smile but in an expression of surprise which at another time would have been ludicrous. Roger actually saw his big nose twitch as he sniffed, saw his lips form the word "petrol."

Lampard said: "My God!"

Morgan squeezed into the room, taking a knife from his pocket and beginning to cut the scarf away from Mark's head. Lampard started on Roger, and Morgan finished with Mark and turned to Harrington.

· · · ·

Detective Sergeant Sloane of Scotland Yard replaced the receiver and looked across at a fellow sergeant. He scratched the end of his nose, and said deliberately:

"They aren't half going some. We've got to get Clay. There's a general call. I wonder what he's been doing!"

"Stop wondering, and get busy," said the other. "Where's Handsome?"

"At Kingston. A rum show," said Sloane, and lifted a telephone to give further orders in an urgent yet curiously deliberate voice.

Earlier, there had been a look-out for Charlie Clay; now there was a hunt to outdo all manhunts.

Next morning Roger was feeling better after the shock at Kingston, but it would be a long time before he forgot the few minutes while all three of them had been helpless.

He had talked to Harrington, who had been just as badly shaken.

Back at the Yard, he received a summons to Chatworth's office.

Chatworth wasn't smiling.

"Sit down," he said. "Smoke if you want to—or don't you feel much like fire and smoke?"

"I shall never like the smell of petrol again," Roger said feelingly. "Thank you, sir." He lit up.

"How's Lessing?"

"He's all right, sir."

"Harrington?"

"It shook him pretty badly. There isn't any doubt that Clay meant to kill the three of us, including Harrington," went on Roger, "and that seems to take the pressure off Harrington."

"You mean, he's no longer on the short list of suspects?"

"He's lower down the list, anyway," Roger replied. "Everything he's told me and everything Garielle Transom's told me stand up to investigation. I've been studying the reports until I know them off by heart. I believe it was a chance of a kind which brought Harrington and Miss Transom together—chance in the sense that she happened to be there when he went to ask for financial help a year or so ago." When Chatworth nodded, Roger knew that he also had made a study of the reports. "I've checked with the Ministry of Defence. Harrington's one of their white-haired boys. He's passed through all the security screens because so much of his work is on the secret list. So—the question is, why should anyone want to murder him?"

Chatworth said: "Two possible motives, eh? Because he stands to inherit *Dreem*. Or because he's doing this hush-hush work. Don't think there are any signs of enemy action here, do you?"

"I think we ought to pass all the information to MI5, sir, through the Special Branch."

"Hoped you'd say that," said Chatworth. "I will. But what's your opinion?"

"I haven't formed a clear-cut one yet, sir. I certainly don't think I've distinguished myself in this so far."

"There's time," said Chatworth, in tacit agreement. "This running with the hare and chasing with the hounds has its problems, hasn't it?"

"Big ones yes," Roger admitted. "On the other hand there are things which Lessing can do which I can't. He can prod Potter much harder, for instance—if I worked on Potter as Lessing does, you would have the Home Secretary breathing down your neck. I can't say I like the situation, but it's as good a way of working as any, at the moment. And Lessing doesn't take unnecessary chances. He uses Pep Morgan—"

"So I see," interrupted Chatworth. "And Morgan has been known to be useful to us, hasn't he?"

"Very useful indeed."

"Get on with Lampard all right?"

"Better than I expected. Lampard and Morgan are high on my list at the moment."

"After what happened at Harrington's, I should think so," Chatworth said drily. "Now, about Potter. I see he offered to bribe Lessing, after Lessing did him some service, and when Lessing refused Potter seemed to make an attempt to break his neck in a lift. Sure that was Potter?"

"Not absolutely sure. There's evidence that Potter has paid Anderson considerable sums of money over a period of about six months, though. Everything starts from six months ago, including the first Prendergast death."

"One moment," Chatworth purred. "Is there *evidence* that Potter has paid money to Anderson? Or inference?"

"I wouldn't like to go into the witness box about it yet," admitted Roger, "but I think I could prove that Potter and Anderson have exchanged money and information. Three times Anderson has left Potter's office, and gone straight to a bank in the Strand. Each time he has deposited two hundred pounds in notes. The time of his calls on Potter have been checked, also the time of his banking of the money. He's had no time to go any-where else but the bank. The notes can't be traced back to Pot-ter, but—"

"That's good enough," said Chatworth. "You're not in the box yet. What has Anderson sold to Potter?"

"Information about the Harrington process, presumably."

"*All* of it?"

Roger smiled.

"He didn't know the whole secret. Harrington has been care-ful, and there's one vital ingredient which Anderson didn't know about. There is more evidence, sir. At Anderson's lodgings there is a notebook containing various items, some marked in red. I've assumed that the marked items are those that he hasn't passed on to Potter, those unmarked were still to be sold." He paused.

"Go on," said Chatworth.

"I think it's possible that Potter decided not to buy anything more from Anderson, who didn't like the decision. I imagine that Anderson tried to blackmail Potter, who struck back. That would make Anderson sore, to say the least. As far as I can see Anderson attacked Potter, and this is the one motive which fits. Of course, Anderson might have been hired—as Clay is. But I think Potter has tried this and failed. He certainly didn't hire Anderson for the attack on himself. That attack was too realis-tic."

"Who killed Anderson?" demanded Chatworth.

"I don't know," said Roger. "It might have been one of Pot-ter's men. I can't see the significance of the two motives—get-ting control of *Dreem* and getting the synthetic rubber process. If Potter was aiming to get the synthetic rubber process through Anderson, why did he refuse to string along with An-derson? Did he find another, easier way? The rubber trouble all began when it was obvious that Japan was going to overrun Ma-laya. The crude rubber available here would be next to nothing for a long time, whether we regained the territory or not. Har-rington's process suddenly became of vital importance and great value. The *Dreem* directors might have decided to try to get in on Harringtons Limited, through Potter."

"Any reason for thinking this way?"

"Transom virtually admitted he wanted a business," said Roger. "He didn't specify what the business was. None of the *Dreem* people could approach Harrington direct very easily, especially Transom. He had antagonized Harrington too much. Potter was working through Anderson to get the process for *Dreem* directors. It looks as if he changed his mind."

"Yes," murmured Chatworth. "Clear enough. Even probable. What does Potter say about his association with Anderson?"

"That Anderson wanted to borrow money from him," said Roger. "It's plausible. Potter does a bit of money-lending on the side. Not officially, but that's what it amounts to. I haven't badgered Potter too much," Roger added, "but he's watched wherever he goes, and he doesn't go to many places. I think we have him worried. I think he ordered Clay to put paid to the three of us at Kingston, and that when it failed he saw the red light. But he's not finished yet."

"Shouldn't think so," agreed Chatworth. "Well, that's all right as far as it goes, but it hardly covers the Prendergast business, nor this new wife, what do you call her? Maisie. What is her association with Potter?"

"We haven't found out yet," admitted Roger.

"Have you any ideas?"

"Ideas is hardly the word, sir, but there are some peculiar things. For instance, Potter was supposed to have 'discovered' Harrington as a relation, whereas in fact Harrington went to see the Prendergasts himself, two years or more ago. They knew he existed, although they gave us to understand that there were no more relatives than those we knew. Then Maisie Prendergast suggested that Harrington wasn't the McCoy. It could be a straw in the wind, indicating that Potter is going to try to refute Harrington's proof of identity."

"Is it possible?"

"His birth certificate seemed in order," said Roger. "I'm a bit doubtful of the passport, it isn't quite a hundred per cent. I've seen some excellent forgeries, and I'm going to have Eddie Day have a look at it." Roger paused.

"Go on," urged Chatworth.

"If we're to assume that Potter planned the murders of the Prendergasts in order to put Maisie, through Claude, in control of *Dreem*," said Roger, "we have a strong enough motive—or we did have until Claude and Maisie started to come to blows. Although the woman has talked a lot in her sleep, there's nothing in the way of evidence against her. She married Claude for his money, yes. He then had two thousand a year, and that's a comfortable income. We can guess all we like, but we've no evidence to support a belief that Maisie knew Claude would soon come into much more money. So—" he raised his hands, for emphasis. "Potter backs Maisie, we *think*. We also think that Potter finds a 'new' relative. Potter contrives to poison Claude, who doesn't die. But supposing Potter is aiming to get the *Dreem* money out of Claude's control and into someone's much more amenable, and Harrington is an obvious choice. But if Potter didn't think Harrington would be pliable—well, sir, what is he likely to do, if he's the criminal I've made out?"

"This is your story, I wouldn't rob you of the climax for the world!"

"Thank you, sir. As far as I can see, Potter would have a stooge impersonate Harrington. That's what I meant by Maisie's straw in the wind. She deliberately gave us the idea, and I imagine Potter put her up to it. It may sound fantastic, but—"

"Not fantastic at all," declared Chatworth swiftly. "Hardly commonplace, perhaps, but there is nothing commonplace about Potter. What does Lessing think about it?"

"You've had a summary of what we both think, sir, as far as we can go. That Potter has his fingers in two very profitable pies. *Dreem*, and Harrington's rubber process."

"Yes. But Potter must know that if he makes a slip, we'll hang him," Chatworth objected.

"He could be under pressures himself."

"You think he is being forced into this?"

"If he could make a big killing and get out of the country to spend it, I'd think he was taking a chance. But he can't. And I can't imagine that he would take such chances just for what he can get out of it, knowing that all the time he's using his money, we're waiting to catch him out."

"See what you mean," said Chatworth. "So, someone might be using pressure on Potter. I've wondered about that myself. Glad to know we agree on the possibility." He smiled, broadly. "Keep at it, West. Don't hesitate to do whatever you think best. We mustn't let Potter get away."

He wandered off into trivialities before dismissing Roger, who went back stimulated if confused. Chatworth had told him as clearly as he could that he, Roger, had *carte blanche*. The cry was "Get Potter," the inference "don't give a damn how!"

Eddie Day was sitting at his desk with a watchmaker's glass screwed in his eye. He put down the cheque he was examining and glanced sideways at Roger, saying hopefully:

"Is the Old Boy in a bad mood today?"

"No worse than usual," said Roger mendaciously. "Are you up for an interview?"

"Gawd help us, no. I wondered, that's all. Sloane looked in just now. I said you'd ring him when you got back."

"Thanks." Roger glanced at his watch. It was nearly half-past one, but Sloane often went late to lunch. He lifted the telephone.

"West speaking," he said.

"Glad you called, sir. I've got something about Clay." There was excitement in Sloane's voice. "He's been found, sir, with the other man. Both dead, both shot in the forehead." Sloane drew in an audible breath. *"They were in a sand pit near Yew House."*

16

BODIES IN A SAND PIT

With a sick feeling in the pit of his stomach, Roger telephoned Chatworth. That was half an hour later, and he had been working at pressure ever since the news from Sloane.

"*Both* dead," Chatworth exploded. "Why in hell didn't you make sure it couldn't happen? My God, what do we have a police force for?" All his amiability was gone. Roger could imagine that his face looked brick red. "It's got to stop—damn it, we *needed* those men. They were the only two we could make talk about Potter. Didn't you realize that?"

"Only too well, sir."

"Know who killed them?"

"No, sir. We know that Potter's been in London all morning, Harrington has been at his work, and Miss Transom on duty. We haven't full reports on the directors of *Dreem*, but Lampard tells me that as far as he knows Claude Prendergast and his wife have been at Delaware all the time. Claude's about again. Lampard's men are stretched pretty thin, though."

"Ought to have sent our men there," growled Chatworth. "Every director of that company must be watched every minute. See to it."

It was useless to talk about manpower shortage.

"Yes, sir."

"And see to it quick." Chatworth rang off.

Roger saw Eddie Day watching him, as if divining Chatworth's mood.

"He after your blood?" asked Eddie, lasciviously.

"Proper vampire, Chatworth," Roger replied. He telephoned Mark. "Mark, I'm going down to Guildford right away. Clay and the little man have been killed. Coming?"

"*Am* I!"

"Pick you up at Victoria Station," Roger said.

"I don't know that I think it's wise to use amateurs," Day said, plaintively.

"We're too short-handed, Eddie. Blame Hitler." Roger lifted the telephone again, and spoke to a messenger. "Get me some meat sandwiches, wrapped up, and take them out to my car, will you? In five minutes." He knew it would take ten.

He picked up his murder bag, always at the ready, told the operator to tell Lampard that he was on his way, and went out to his car. The messenger soon came hurrying with a big packet of sandwiches.

"And I thought you'd like a bottle of beer, sir." He took one out of his tunic pocket.

"Good idea," Roger said. "Telephone my wife, will you? Tell her I may be late tonight."

"I will, sir."

He picked Mark up ten minutes later, and told him what Chatworth had said as they drove down to Guildford.

Most of the drive they were silent.

By a stile in the hedge bordering Yew House was a uniformed policeman, who recognized Roger, and saluted.

"Is Inspector Lampard still here?" Roger did not get out of the car.

"Yes, sir. I believe he's in a summerhouse at the back of the garden here. You can get to it this way. It's quicker than going by the drive."

They parked the car, and walked over rough grassland.

Lampard was busy in the wooden summerhouse. He had utilized an old table as a desk, and had papers spread all over it. Not far away were two bodies covered with sheeting.

Lampard looked up, half-smiled a greeting, and plunged into detail immediately. The two men had been found in the first instance by a Home Guard, who had been on duty near the spot, and noticed a smell. It had now been decided that the two men had been dead for at least twelve hours. Tenby had been to the pit and had been reasonably sure of that. In case Roger wanted to see him, the doctor would be at Delaware during the evening; he was calling to see Claude.

"Thanks," said Roger.

Lampard went on, accepting philosophically that the two men had been killed within hours, possibly within two or three hours, of leaving the Kingston flat after the attempt at a triple-murder.

There was nothing helpful in the men's pockets, and no indication, yet, as to whether they had been killed in the quarry or taken there after death. The probability was that they had been killed there, since there was no sign of bruises and had they been dead when they reached the spot it was likely that they would have been thrown over the edge.

Lampard took a small envelope from the table.

"Tenby got one of the bullets," he said, and rolled it on to a sheet of paper. "Here's the one that killed Anderson." He rolled that out of another envelope. "I'll have it checked, but I think they're the same gun. I've had half-a-dozen men brought here, to watch the house," he added. "Mr. and Mrs. Transom are in, but no one else except the servants."

"What's Transom's attitude?" Mark asked.

"Shocked," said Lampard, and rubbed his chin while he looked at Roger. "We're about two miles from Delaware," he added slowly. "That's a bullet from a small gun. A woman could use it, couldn't she?"

Roger was startled. "A woman?"

156

"Good Lord," said Mark suddenly, making Roger look at him and away from Lampard. "Of course. A woman could use a light-calibre all right. Can you think of anyone, Roger, or is the mind quite blank?"

Roger had a vision of Maisie Prendergast, who was nearby at Delaware House.

. . . .

The three men in the summerhouse were silent for a few moments.

Then Roger asked:

"Has the little man been identified yet?"

"No," replied Lampard.

"Let's call him Smith. We know that Clay and Smith ran away from Harrington's flat to what they considered a place of safety. They were shot by someone waiting for them. The rendezvous must surely have been arranged before. The probability is that they were either coming here or going to their headquarters via the quarry."

"There's one other possible place, apart from Delaware House," Lampard said. "It's called The Gables, and lies about a mile north of Yew House."

"Who lives there?"

"No one in any way connected with this affair as far as I can discover," said Lampard. "A Mr. Clement Delaroy. Old, uncommunicative, unfriendly and, I believe, a brilliant economist in his youth. He's been there for some five years, and no one knows a great deal about him. In case you're thinking that five years is a comparatively short time, only two people have lived in this particular part of the district for more. The Prendergasts and the Transoms. Most of the others are new-comers since the bombing of London started. Delaroy is a comparatively old resident, although locals see little of him. He shops in the village or in Guildford, employs local servants, but bars his land to anyone and is constantly asking for prosecutions under the Trespass Laws."

Mark rubbed his chin.

"All you want to tell us now is that he wears a big grey beard and wig, and the grounds of his house have gone to rack and ruin. Then we'll have our man of mystery, and just be able to go along and arrest him. It couldn't work out like that, of course?"

"He's quite bald," said Lampard. "His garden is the loveliest thing you're ever likely to see. Before the war he employed three full-time gardeners in his four acres. There is nothing mysterious about Delaroy. He only comes into the picture because his rear fence is less than a mile from the sand pit where we found the bodies. His is one of the gardens where the soil is very sandy, too."

"Sandy soil, incomparable garden?" Mark made the words a question.

"He brought in a lot of soil from the other side of the village," Lampard said. "Purely as a precaution I'm having the house watched, but I'm not really hopeful of any results from there. The probabilities are surely that the killer came from Yew House or Delaware House, but I want to get back to Guildford to check on these and other things." He picked up the rifle bullets, and stood up. "Will you go to see Transom?"

"Yes," said Roger.

"I had a call just before you came—Harrington and Garielle Transom are up there. You might play one off against the other."

"Worth trying," Roger agreed.

"Still room for a passenger?" asked Mark.

"I'd better carry you along," said Roger. "We'll walk up. The car's as well here as any place."

They cut across the grounds towards Yew House, approaching it from the side, and seeing a small car standing outside the front door. Neither of them recognized it, but as they went towards the head of the drive along a gravel path which led past one side of Yew House, they heard a voice raised in anger. Two others, both feminine, were apparently trying to soothe the speaker.

The speaker was Transom; even in a rage he could not wholly discard his pompous manner.

"A stop by the way is indicated," said Mark. "Much could come out in a family row." Shrubs hid them from sight of the house although they could see the large window, and against it Transom, standing sideways towards them and facing someone hidden in the shadows of the room.

"For the first and the last time," Transom said in a quivering voice, "I will not have you in my house! Be quiet, Clara! Garielle, I will not have another word from you on this subject. I have given my decision, and you will either abide by it, or—"

"I don't think you quite know what you're doing," Garielle said clearly. "Hadn't you better think more about it?"

"I have thought too much!" shouted Transom. "Now, sir, must I call my servants to show you to the door?"

"If he goes, father, I go too," said Garielle.

"You may please yourself. It has been your habit for the past two years, and I am not impressed by where it has taken you." Transom made a choking noise in his throat. "I little thought that the day would come when my own daughter would admit that she had made a habit of spending the night—*nights!*—with a man whom she met casually, a man who—oh, I have talked enough! Your past mistakes will be forgiven, if—"

Harrington broke in calmly.

"You know, Mr. Transom, I've heard of people like you, read about them and seen them on the screen, but I didn't think they existed. If a young woman of twenty-five wants to go as she pleases, it's the usual thing to allow her to. Even if you think she's mixing with a sex-fiend, do you imagine this is the way to stop her? You're so hidebound in your Victorianism that I can't imagine how you live in this sordid world. But apart from moral scruples, where's your faith in Garielle? You're implying that she's no better than a whore. I don't like that innuendo about my wife."

. . . .

"How about *that*," Mark whispered.

"Quiet," breathed Roger.

It was deathly quiet, after Harrington stopped, and the silence lasted until someone began to breathe heavily. Then came little clucking sounds, probably from Clara Transom.

Transom exploded:

"Your *wife!* Garielle, he can't mean that! It can't be true. You haven't married this mountebank! I can't believe it, I won't believe it!"

"Will a marriage certificate convince you?" asked Garielle, and a rustling of paper sounded. "Would you like to see it now?" She spoke as if it was all she could do to stop herself from shouting. The tension in the room must be at breaking point.

"Why does Transom hate Harrington?" Mark could not keep quiet.

"We'll find out."

Clara Transom exclaimed:

"Oh, Garry, Garry. Why, why did you have to deceive us!"

"Because if I hadn't father would have tried to stop our wedding," Garielle said evenly. "There would have been another horrible outburst in the newspapers. Do you think I want my affairs put in the headlines because my father's a crank on the subject of women? A dozen times—a *hundred* times!—I've asked him why he objected to the man I love. He's never tried to answer it. He's always put me off by saying that he wanted someone better for me. *Better!*" Her scorn was scathing. "He would like to lead me to the altar with some ape with a title. Look at the specimens he's had here to parade in front of me!"

After a short silence, Transom said:

"No, it wasn't that, Garielle." His voice was low-pitched, a most surprising thing. "I wished you to marry well, my dear, but I desired your happiness above all things. I knew that you could never be happy with this fraud. He is no more William Harrington than I am. He is no relative of the Prendergasts, he has simply pretended to be in order to get the *Dreem* company. But what can I do now? What *can* I do?"

Garielle said: "Daddy, you must believe—"

"It cannot be forgotten," Transom said.

There was an edge to Harrington's voice. "Who put this idea into your head, Mr. Transom? If those policemen—"

"It has nothing to do with the police. When I knew that you were associating with my daughter I made inquiries. I received positive proof that you are not Harrington. Your name is Duke Conroy." Transom was speaking with an obvious effort, and there were long pauses between some of the words. "I had documentary proof of this. I was prevailed upon to keep silent because it seemed the wiser course. I never dreamed of this."

"Daddy, it isn't true."

Harrington said: "Who gave you the information?"

"It doesn't matter."

"For better or worse you're my father-in-law," Harrington said sardonically. "I'm not going to be evaded like this. Who was it?"

"His name—" began Transom.

Abruptly, without the slightest warning, a *crack!* sounded behind Roger and Mark, the sound of a rifle shot. Something hummed past them. It struck Transom on the side of the head. There was a short, devastating silence before Roger and Mark swung round.

As they turned they caught a glimpse of a man not twenty yards behind them, his face hidden by a slouch hat pulled low.

Roger shouted, and dropped to his knees. Mark followed. A bullet whanged over their heads and struck the wall of Yew House. Roger rose to his knees cautiously, hearing movements ahead of him. He saw the man who had now turned away from them; the top of his rifle showed above his head. He was racing towards a thicker belt of trees.

"Careful, Roger!"

Mark drew an automatic from his pocket as he straightened

up. The man's hat and the top of the rifle continued to show. From somewhere farther to the north came the shrill blast of a police whistle, but it was too far away to offer any direct threat to the rifleman.

Mark fired, aiming low. The bullet lost itself amongst the shrubs, and the man ran on. Mark moved towards a clearer spot, and then caught a glimpse of the other. He fired twice, from the hip, saw the man stagger and sway forward, only to recover and go on running. His speed was reduced, but his recuperative powers were good. He swung round, lowering the gun.

He was no more than twenty yards from Mark, and Roger could not see how the man could miss.

Mark squeezed his trigger again, as the rifle spoke. Its bullet went hopelessly high, while Mark's hit the rifleman in the chest. The man coughed, then dropped his rifle. As he crumpled up, his face was hidden. They saw only that he was a small man.

He sprawled forward on his face.

Behind Roger and Mark, Harrington came running, and close on his heels came Garielle. From the shrubs to the north of the house two policemen broke into sight, running hard but at first purposelessly. Then they saw the others and headed towards them.

From the open window a scream was coming, a high-pitched, unremitting scream.

Harrington stopped and said to Garielle:

"Go to her, Garry."

Garielle turned and went back to the house.

Mark and Roger were the first to bend over the wounded man, a man who might be dead. Roger went on one knee and removed his hat; and then stared down at an old, lined face, at grey hair, and lips which were working in pain.

An echo of Janet's voice was in Roger's ears.

"He's rather a dear," she had said. *"He's rather a dear."*

There he was, coughing now and with his face twisted, the rifle not a yard from him, and the evidence of Roger and Mark to convict him of the attack on Transom if nothing else. It was Petrie, the Prendergasts' servant.

"He's rather a dear," Janet had said. *"He's rather a dear."*

. . . .

Lampard's men couldn't be blamed for letting this old man go wherever he wished. No one could be blamed—but another director of *Dreem* was dead.

17

ONE BY ONE

Roger walked slowly from the study at Delaware into the lounge. It was empty, and there was no fire. The darkness of evening spread over the countryside, but the blackout was not drawn, and there was a little light in the big room, although it was full of shadows. From outside there came the sound of birds, settling for the night, and from inside the sharp rattle of curtains being pulled across rails.

Roger stood by the window, looking out, and was there when the door opened and a woman appeared.

"May—may I do the blackout, sir, please?"

"Yes," said Roger. He turned from the window, and caught a glimpse of the sight he had been waiting for: the gleam of car lights coming along the drive. He was on the porch to receive Lampard and Mark, who climbed out of the Guildford Inspector's car hurriedly.

"Well, that's that," said Mark. "The same gun without a doubt. Same markings on the bullets that killed Anderson, Clay, 'Smith' and Transom. Petrie was the rifleman, and he's on what the hospital calls the danger list." Mark paused, then added: "It's said he'd never used a gun until he joined the Home Guard."

Roger nodded, and Lampard stepped through into the hall, taking off his hat.

There was a sense of anti-climax about the arrival, although the news that Petrie was alive was welcome.

"I've been through his papers," Roger said. "There's nothing there to indicate why he did it, or that he's involved with Potter or anyone else. He's worked for the family for twenty-three years. It doesn't make sense. None of the case makes sense. There's murder after murder, and nothing we can do to prevent it. We're within ten yards of him and we let Transom die. We're no farther on than we were when we started. Or have you been gifted with a vision?" he demanded sourly.

"No visions," said Mark. "No self-reproach either. I haven't any ideas in the back of my head. If I had, Petrie wouldn't have worried me. How's Maisie?"

"All she says is that she doesn't believe it," Roger reported. "Claude's conscious, but I haven't told him yet. He's much better," he added, as if he was searching for something good to say. "At least we've saved his life. Others could be more valuable."

"I think we should get to Yew House again," Lampard said. "Wade has been there alone too long on his own already."

"Yes," said Roger. "Mark, you stay here and keep an eye on Maisie and Claude. I don't feel that anyone's safe now. You'll be shooting me next," he added, and then suddenly laughed, with a slight easing of his depression. "Five more minutes like that and I'll be asking for a nice safe job as a fighter pilot. Ready, Lampard?"

The telephone bell cut across Lampard's "yes".

Roger reached it, to hear the bright voice of Inspector Wade.

"May I speak to Mr. Lampard, please?"

"Hold on." Roger put the receiver of the old-type instrument into Lampard's hand. Wade's voice crackled without making sense to Roger and Mark, but it did not last for long. Lampard replaced the receiver, and looked round.

"Widdison and Hauteby have just arrived at Yew House," he announced. "It's certainly time we went there."

It took them twenty minutes to reach Transom's. Outside Harrington's car was dwarfed by a Daimler with a chauffeur leaning inelegantly against one corner. He straightened up as the two policemen arrived, but eyed them vacantly.

A servant opened the door.

"Mr. Harrington said, sir, would you please go to Mr.—Mr. Transom's study?" There were tears in the woman's eyes, and she sniffed as she finished.

"Thank you," said Lampard, and led the way upstairs.

Roger had seen little of the big hall and the wide gallery. He had a feeling that he had stepped out of the present into the past, but he paid little attention to the hall or the gallery as he followed Lampard to the room where a sliver of light showed under the door. Lampard tapped, and entered.

Harrington was standing with his back to the fireplace, Hauteby and Widdison were sitting on either side of the fire, while in the background Wade hovered, shiny-faced and smiling. Roger had expected to see Garielle, but she was not there.

"Hallo," said Harrington. "I thought you'd be back earlier."

"We couldn't make it," said Lampard.

Roger studied Widdison and Hauteby. Widdison looked a much older man than his years, his face was wizened and his eyebrows jutted; the word "ogre" was at least justified by appearance. His face was brick red. His eyes were buried in deep sockets, and his mouth appeared to be shrivelled, so that a set of dentures showed plainly: large, ugly dentures, also revealing his gums.

Hauteby was a dark man, dark-skinned, dark-eyed, black-haired. He was dressed immaculately, his hair brushed sleekly from his high, smooth forehead. One of a type, Roger thought, whereas Widdison was certainly unique.

They were the only remaining directors of *Dreem*, Claude excepted.

"Your man asked us not to look through any papers," Harrington said. "We've obeyed instructions." There was a note of sarcasm in his voice, but he looked tired. "Did you get the man identified?"

Widdison leaned forward.

"That's right. Who was it?"

"Petrie, the servant of the Prendergasts," Lampard said.

"Good God!" gasped Widdison. His voice croaked, there was bewilderment in his expression which looked convincing. "Petrie, the old snake! Why, he's been—"

"He's been a servant of the family for many years," said Roger. The keenness of his voice made Lampard stare. "Not a man one would expect to go suddenly killer-crazy. He's certainly killed three people whom he might have believed were parties to murdering the Prendergasts, the family he has served for so long."

"Good God!" exclaimed Widdison again; it was a blasphemy.

"Have you any reason for suggesting that?" Hauteby's eyes were restless as they looked at Roger.

"The obvious one," Roger said, concealing the fact that the idea had come almost with the words. "What other motive could there be?" The idea had come when he had realized who the rifleman was. He needed time to investigate it more thoroughly, and he came out with it because it would obviously worry both Widdison and Hauteby. "What brought you here, gentlemen?"

"We were told of the murder," Hauteby said. "We came to offer sympathy and help to Mrs. Transom. If—if Petrie thought *we* killed his employers . . . but why should he?"

"You had a meeting here the other night with a Mr. Gabriel Potter," Roger said. "Sir Andrew McFallen was to have been here, but he was killed. I understand that Potter rejected a proposition which you put to him. It is possible that the murders are connected with that proposition. I want to know exactly what it was."

Widdison croaked: "Damned if you will!"

"Are we to take that as a refusal to co-operate with the police?" Lampard demanded.

"Take it as what you like," said Widdison. "It's our business. Nothing to do with you or anyone else."

Roger said:

"Mr. Harrington, when you were talking to me last night you promised to advise your backer that we wanted to know who had financed you. Have you done that?"

"Yes," said Harrington.

"Are you prepared to disclose his name?"

"He refused permission."

Lampard said: "There are limits to the obstruction which we can permit, Mr. Harrington. You may have promised not to disclose the name of your backer, but that is unimportant compared with the issues now."

Harrington looked at him stubbornly.

Widdison and Hauteby turned from Roger to Lampard, as if uncertain from whom to expect the next question. In a detached fashion Roger thought that he had perfected this dual role with Mark, but had not expected Lampard to slip so easily into the habit. It served the purpose of confusing the others, of adding to their uncertainty; and there was nervousness here as well as apprehension. There was nothing normal about the reactions of any of them, Harrington possibly excepted, and Harrington had kept far too many facts to himself.

· Hauteby said: "I don't think there is any reason why I shouldn't tell you, Inspector. Mr. Transom backed Harringtons Limited."

"What?"

"Oh no, he didn't," said Harrington. "You did."

Now it was coming out. Lampard had known what to expect. Hauteby and Harrington glared at one another, while Widdison made a clicking noise with his false teeth.

"You thought it was me, Harrington," Hauteby said. "You will remember that I told you that I had not sufficient capital myself, but that I thought I could induce someone else to put it up. I did. Transom financed you seventy-five per cent. I did the rest."

"But I thought I was poison to him!"

"So you were," said Hauteby. "But he was not fool enough to allow personal dislike to interfere with business. After he had thought over your proposition, he saw its possibilities. So did I. Neither of us wanted the other directors to have any share, so Transom put up most of the money, and I supplied the rest."

Widdison kept clicking his teeth; so far as it was possible for him to look anything but grotesque, he looked angry.

"All right," said Roger. "We now know who financed you, Mr. Harrington, but we don't know why you wanted to keep Mr. Hauteby's name out of it."

"He made it a condition," Harrington said. "In any case the process is on the secret list, and I had strict orders from the Ministry of Supply to keep it that way. I was puzzled by the things that were happening, and wanted to sit back and watch them work out. I knew that there were people trying to discredit me, and I thought that it was the family and probably the other *Dreem* directors. It looked like an effort to get rid of me, and take over the process. That wasn't an idea I wanted to put up to you, though. I thought the police were there to find the answers, not to be spoon fed. I preferred to look on," he added. "I might have taken a different view but for my wife. I wanted the marriage kept quiet, too. But there was queer business all along the line, and I intended to find out who was behind it." He paused, and put his pipe between his teeth. "Take it or leave it," he said, "I had no other motive."

"Hadn't you, darling?" asked Garielle.

She came in from the door, which had opened quietly. Her face was pale, but pallor could not rob her blue eyes of their brightness, nor affect the beauty of her movements. She had changed from Air Force blue to lemon-coloured two-piece with a white blouse, frilly at the front.

Harrington said: "Garry, you don't want to—"

"I do want to," interrupted Garielle Harrington. "I'm tired of it all, darling. We can't go on being fools." She looked at Roger. "Bill was vague and obstructive because I wanted him to be. I told you that we had met by accident for the same reason."

It was a fact, reflected Roger, that there was no sound in the room but her quiet voice. Every eye was turned towards her, every face held an expression of tense anticipation. It was more than the fact that everyone looked towards the speaker, more than the effect of an exceptionally beautiful woman on an audience of men. The inflection in her voice hinted at revelations, but there was even more to it than that. It was as if Hauteby, Widdison, and Harrington were afraid of what those revelations might be.

Harrington said nothing.

"I persuaded him to be evasive with his story. I persuaded him to keep you guessing. And I helped him all I could. You see, although I had quarrelled with my father, he was still my father. I thought he might be involved in all the crimes. I knew he was working with the man Potter, and I've heard of Potter's reputation. Father was afraid, too. He lived with that kind of fear which dogs a man everywhere, and which he can't hide no matter how hard he tries. I thought that he was deliberately trying to ruin Bill because of his objections to our association, but I couldn't accept it. I didn't try to rationalize my ideas, they were vivid impressions and deep fears. Something was going on underneath the surface, and I did all I could to make sure that you didn't suspect my father. I thought he would realize that whatever he was doing would have to stop once the police were in it. It was a case of divided loyalties, Inspector. Bill backed me up. It's as simple as that."

She went over to Harrington, and slipped an arm through his. He pressed her to his side, and smiled down with a twisted but reassuring smile. They looked quite homely outlined against the dull red fire.

Lampard broke the silence.

"You suspected your father of some kind of criminal enterprise, Mrs. Harrington. Do you still maintain that you had no idea what it was?"

"Except that it involved my husband, I knew and I know nothing," said Garielle. "But I can tell you one thing. Father had some papers hidden in the house." She glanced up at a clock fastened to the wall above the mantelpiece, turning her head to do so. "I don't know what they are, but I know that clock can be taken away, and there is a safe behind it. The keys are in amongst those which you took out of father's pocket, Inspector Lampard."

18

DOCUMENTS OF INTEREST

Just as every eye had been turned towards Garielle, they now turned towards the clock. It was an oak-faced, intricately carved example of an early Georgian clock-maker's art. Its loud ticking could be heard in every corner of the room; the ticks were exaggerated by the tension.

Lampard said: "How did you come to know about this?"

"Mother has just told me," said Garielle. "It's time we knew the worst, I think. Or the best." For the first time she allowed some feelings to show, and she bit her underlip. Then she took a grip on herself, while Lampard turned to Wade.

"Where are the keys, Wade?"

"Here, sir." Wade took a small attaché case from the floor at the side of Transom's desk.

Lampard opened the case, pulled out a piece of dark cloth, unfolded it, and spread the contents of Transom's pockets on the desk. A leather key-case was amongst them. He picked this up and opened it.

"Do you know which key, Mrs. Harrington?"

"I'm afraid not."

Hauteby and Widdison were sitting forward in their chairs, staring at Lampard. The tension was almost red hot.

Lampard crossed to the mantelpiece. Harrington and Garielle moved aside so that he could get to the clock more easily. The clock did not shift at the first attempt, but Lampard persisted, and eventually found the secret. He pressed a piece of the carved woodwork, which released a spring which held the timepiece close to the wall. It came away on a hinge. Behind it was a round wall-safe, with a sunken handle. The keyhole was on the right-hand side.

Roger was studying the *Dreem* directors. Widdison had his hands tight on the arm of his chair, and Hauteby was sitting bolt upright. Harrington and Garielle, nearest Lampard, were looking at him with an interest only a little less tense. Wade was gaping, as Lampard began to try the keys, one after another, showing no signs of tension or excitement.

The fifth key fitted. Lampard turned it.

There was an audible gasp from Widdison, and Hauteby shifted in his chair. Roger glanced away. Lampard was lifting something from the safe. He had a sealed envelope in his right hand, and explored the inside of the safe for anything else; apparently there was nothing, for he withdrew his hand.

"This seems to be it."

Hauteby moved again.

He did two things at the same time, standing up and taking his right hand from his pocket. The electric light shone on the barrel of an automatic. He backed swiftly towards the wall alongside Lampard; it was the only place which he could reach quickly while keeping the whole company covered.

Wade drew a hissing breath.

Roger saw the red-faced Inspector out of the corner of his eye. Wade was picking up the attache case, obviously preparing to throw it. Hauteby fired a single shot. The bullet buried itself in Wade's shoulder, and the case dropped with a clatter to the ground. Wade clutched his shoulder, but stood staring, swaying.

The echoes of the shot floated about the room.

"Give me that envelope," Hauteby said harshly. "Put it on the arm of my chair."

Lampard's grip tightened on the envelope.

"I've warned you," Hauteby said. His face was twisted, his

lips drawn together in a thin line. "I mean to have it. Don't throw your life away."

Roger wondered if it were really happening, whether it was possible that the man seriously expected to get away with the envelope. Other police were downstairs, more in the garden; the shot must have been heard. There was no sound but the heavy breathing of the men and Garielle.

Lampard threw the envelope into Hauteby's face.

Hauteby thrust up his left hand and snatched the envelope out of the air, then shot out his right foot as Lampard came forward. A crunching sound came as his foot went into Lampard's stomach. Lampard groaned and sank down. Hauteby slewed the gun round towards the others, saying:

"Get near Widdison, all of you."

"Don't," Garielle exclaimed suddenly. "Bill, don't, it's useless!"

Roger saw Harrington's hands clench, knew that the girl expected him to rush at Hauteby. If Harrington did it would be suicide.

He had to get that gun and make sure no one was hurt. He had to make Hauteby drop both the gun and envelope, to make the effort which Wade and Lampard had already tried, so disastrously. It gave him a numbness in the pit of his stomach, especially as Harrington and Garielle moved back towards Widdison's chair, and Hauteby turned to him. The man was ruthless. He meant to get away with that envelope, and did not care what he had to do to achieve it.

"I'll give you thirty seconds," Hauteby said.

Roger swallowed a lump in his throat.

"I don't know that I need that long."

This was the moment he had to make his move. His mind was curiously void of fear. Police outside should be here by now, it was as if this case had a jinx. What a way to take charge! He took a step towards Widdison's chair, and stumbled over the edge of a skin rug. He straightened up, as Hauteby's gun

174

moved. Hauteby did not press the trigger, or utter further threats, but the stumble had helped—he thought Roger had lost his chance.

Roger stumbled again, and fell.

He was on the ground, when he saw the stab of flame from Hauteby's gun. The crack of the shot was loud in his ears, a dull plop came as the bullet buried itself in the floor ahead of him. He rolled over towards Hauteby. Harrington shot out a hand and swept the ornaments from the mantelpiece towards the man with the gun. A vase struck Hauteby's shoulder, as a second bullet nicked Roger's arm.

Hauteby was off his balance, and slewed his gun round towards Harrington, but Harrington was on him in a flash. The crack of his fist on Hauteby's chin echoed nearly as loudly as the pistol shots.

Harrington saw Hauteby's gun arm fly upwards, and he seized the man's wrist. The gun dropped as Roger began to pick himself up slowly, scowling because of the pain in his arm. Hauteby was stretched out, unconscious, and the gun and the letter were in Harrington's hand.

"Got 'em both," Roger remarked absurdly.

"Got them both," said Harrington. "I'd like to break this swine's neck." He bent down and lifted Hauteby bodily, then dropped him into the chair. He pressed a bell-push by the side of the mantelpiece. "Where the hell are your men?"

"If you'll raise a shout on the landing, someone will come," said Roger. "May I have those?" He kept his left arm close to his side, the elbow crooked. There was a throbbing pain half-way between the wrist and elbow, but he did not say that he had been injured.

Harrington handed over the gun and envelope and went into the passage. His bellow echoed back into the room, but there was no answering call, and no one responded to the ringing of the bell in the domestic quarters.

He called: "I'll go and rout 'em out, West."

"We're all right here," said Roger. "Miss Transom, would you mind looking at Wade's shoulder?" He did not want to give Wade any attention himself; he was still afraid that Widdison might have a trick up his sleeve. Widdison had not moved since the threat from Hauteby; he sat back in his chair like a grotesque dummy, his deep-set eyes glowing.

Garielle moved towards Wade, who had dropped into a chair by the desk. Lampard was trying to sit up; he kept his hands pressed tightly against his stomach, and his face was a greyish-green, as if he was suffering from severe air-sickness.

"Take it easy, Lampard," said Roger.

A shout came from Harrington, loud at first then fading away in a gurgle. Garielle swung round from Wade. The cry tapered off into a gasping note, followed by a sudden thudding noise; Roger had a swift vision of Harrington falling down the stairs.

He said to Garielle: "Stay where you are."

He pushed her aside as he reached the door. As he showed himself in the dimly-lighted passage, he saw a flash of flame ahead of him. It showed a glimpse of a huge figure. The bullet smacked into the door, not an inch from him. He fired, but missed, and then from the other end of the passage another bullet struck his shoe.

He backed swiftly into the room.

"Bill, I must go to Bill," cried Garielle. She tried to push past Roger, but he blocked her way. He caught a glimpse of the massive figure again and fired, heard a gasp and thought he had made a hit, but before he could be sure he slammed the door, then turned the key in it. Garielle shot out a hand to get the key, but Roger put it in his pocket, saying:

"You wouldn't get a yard along the passage. Don't act like a fool." He kept the gun in his right hand and went swiftly to the telephone, heard the operator's voice and said: "Tell the Guildford police to send a strong force to Yew House, and give me Mrs. Prendergast's house, Delaware."

He waited for the girl operator to say: "Yes, sir, right away."

He heard the ringing sound, not once but half-a-dozen times. Then came a sudden silence.

"The line's cut," he said, and turned as there was a rap on the door.

A man spoke in a voice he did not recognize.

"Hand out that envelope, West. We'll leave you alone then. You can't get help, the line is cut. I'll give you three minutes."

Lampard had pulled himself up to a sitting position against Hauteby's chair. Widdison crouched back in his, staring at the door, no more life in him than in a corpse. Garielle had stopped glaring and was eyeing Roger with a scared look in her eyes. Wade was slumped over the desk.

Roger said nothing, and the man went on:

"You can't get out. The police have gone, and the servants. The house is empty, except for you—and us. If you don't surrender those papers, West, I'll destroy them. There's only one way of doing that. By fire."

Roger said slowly: "Your last fire wasn't very good."

"This one will be."

Garielle said quietly: "What about the window, Mr. West?"

"Don't show yourself," he ordered. "Pull the curtains back, that will attract attention." She obeyed, while there was another thud on the door. Garielle pulled at the heavy curtains, and they moved without trouble. The light would shine out for miles, but it might be half an hour before anyone took enough notice of it to send word to the authorities. Black-out or no black-out, the house was in comparatively empty country. There was little chance of help coming quickly enough unless the operator had acted promptly.

Garielle passed in front of the window and pulled the other curtain. Outside, it looked very dark. The light from the single electric lamp reflected on the window.

The unfamiliar voice said: "I mean it, West."

Roger kept silent, and into the hush came another report, from outside. A bullet struck the window, shattering the glass.

Widdison gasped, and Garielle backed away. Three reports came in quick succession; on the third a bullet smacked into the light. Darkness fell as slivers of glass were strewn about the room.

Roger stood stock still in the pitch blackness.

"I'll put on the desk-light," Garielle said. "They can't hit that. Don't move. I might knock into you." Roger heard her moving, heard also a movement outside the door. He fancied that he smelt petrol, but could not be sure. His mind was full of the memory of what had happened at Harrington's flat, the horror of those few minutes were made fresh and vivid.

Garielle clicked on the desk lamp.

Its yellow glow spread about the room, but only a small circle of bright light showed, on the desk. It shone on Wade's head— and showed also the pool of blood from the wound in his shoulder. After the *click!* of the light switch the silence was broken only by movements outside. Roger waited, tightening his hold on the envelope.

No further words came.

There was no sound inside or outside the room except the heavy breathing of the occupants. Garielle was staring at Roger, her lips parted. Roger waited for perhaps thirty seconds, then pointed a hand towards the lamp. Garielle was quick to put it out, and he crossed softly towards the door.

19

MARK TAKES A WALK

As Roger moved towards the door he put the envelope into the inside pocket of his coat. He had looked round the room, making sure that no one was within the line of shooting from the door. There was only one course open; he must delay the men outside from putting the threat of fire into operation.

How long would help be? An hour? Only ten minutes had gone.

He turned the key in the lock, with hardly a sound.

He gripped the handle with his right hand, the gun in his left, and, pressing tightly against the wall, opened the door a fraction. A glow of light spread into the room. He caught a glimpse of a shapeless figure carrying a bulky bundle. The bundle hid the other's face, but also prevented him from seeing Roger. It was a sitting target. Roger fired low down and aimed for the walker's thighs.

The bundle dropped. The man turned and fled, gasping. A heavy thud suggested a fall. Roger pushed the door to swiftly. A bullet from the other direction struck its woodwork.

"Did you hit him?" breathed Garielle.

"I think so." Roger heard footsteps padding past the door. He leaned against it and smiled as Garielle put the light on again. "I hope help won't be too long, because—"

He stopped. From the hall there came another shout, more of

surprise than pain. A door banged, a shot barked, footsteps came thundering. It sounded like a dozen men.

There was an outburst of shooting, and then a shouted order in a voice unfamiliar to both of them.

"After him one by one, and keep your distance!"

Footsteps sounded on the stairs, and heavy ones along the passage. They slowed down near the door, and Mark Lessing said:

"Are you around, Roger?"

"Lessing!" exclaimed Garielle.

"Yes, we make a team," Roger said. He was sweating as he opened the door. Mark and a burly man in khaki strode in, the burly man's overcoat sleeve bearing a strip of cloth and the words: *Home Guard.*

Another khaki figure passed the door, heading for the end of the passage.

"So you did get yourself in a jam," said Mark. His grin disappeared as he saw Hauteby, Wade, and Lampard, and he jumped when Garielle hurried past him towards the stairs. The Home Guard officer asked:

"What's got into her?"

"She'll be all right," said Roger. "How many of the crowd have you stopped?"

"Only two or three," said Mark. "The only one outside was the man who fired at your light. I was that side and saw him. Did I thank the fates that there were some Home Guard chaps nearby without prejudice or red tape."

The big officer grinned.

"Cut out the blarney," he said. "But what has been happening here? Have you phoned for a doctor?"

"The phone's cut," said Roger. "We'll have to get to another phone, or send by road. Do any of your men know first aid?"

"Several of them. Good God, it looks as if the invasion's started!"

Two of his men came at the double when he called for them. Roger and Mark left the room and went towards the stairs. By one wall a huddled figure was on the ground. Near it a Home Guard stood with fixed bayonet; it was one of the oddest sights.

"Victim one," said Mark. "It was trying to crawl away, but we intervened. There was another one at the foot of the stairs. I didn't stop to look, but—"

He broke off.

Garielle was on her knees beside the "other heap," cradling Harrington's head in her arms. The light was too dim to show whether he was badly hurt, but as they drew nearer she said:

"How soon can we get an ambulance? He's broken his leg, and I think—I think some ribs." Her voice was low-pitched. "Please don't waste time."

"We won't lose a second," Roger promised.

The Home Guard officer sent a motor-cyclist into Delaware village for a doctor, and with instructions to telephone for Tenby at Guildford. Before the doctors arrived, a dozen policemen in three cars reached Yew House. By then, too, Roger had explained, and the house had been searched. There was no one else there, except the "heap," and Roger said:

"So one of our men got away. Mark, how did you get here? What brought you?"

"I thought you wouldn't be able to wait to ask that much longer," said Mark. "I took a walk."

Again he stopped abruptly, for he could see the "heap" by the head of the stairs. It was Roger's victim. He stank of petrol. Cushions from the lounge, also soaked in petrol, were strewn about the hall. There was no longer any doubt that the house would have been set on fire, and everyone inside burned to death.

Neither Roger nor Mark was thinking of that as they recognized Roger's victim. It was Maisie Prendergast.

. . . .

An hour or so later, the doctors and ambulances had arrived; Wade, Lampard, and Harrington had been taken to hospital with Garielle going in Harrington's ambulance; and a nurse had come for Mrs. Transom. She was in a heavy drugged sleep, after a morphine injection.

In a large woodshed, four frightened servants had been found. They said they had been held up at the point of a gun and forced to go into the shed. The same story was given by the three policemen who had been on duty about the house. All told the same version—a tall, thin man, with a gun, had forced them. At least, there had been no killing for the sake of killing.

Maisie, wounded in the thigh, was on the way to Guildford, also in an ambulance. She either feigned unconsciousness or was genuinely dead to the world, for she could not be made to open her eyes.

"Delaware was pretty grim on my own, and Maisie was staying put in her bedroom," Mark said. "Claude was asleep, with the nurse in his room. A grim sight, that nurse, a raw gaunt Scot. No one would get at Claude with her in the way, I thought, and when Maisie decided to take a walk, so did I. And could she walk! She strode over the hills as if she'd been used to them all her life, and met the tall thin man not far from here. They talked as they walked. I couldn't get near enough to hear them. They met a third man, who had orders to watch the windows of the study, and it looked like a time for reinforcements. I knew the Home Guard were staging night patrol manoeuvres, as someone rang me up to ask if Petrie would be on duty. I persuaded the large lieutenant to lend a hand. We heard the shooting from the grounds when we were half a mile away. I couldn't get here fast enough! I came close to leaving it too late, but it looked as if numbers were called for. Could I have helped any of the others?"

"You did just right," said Roger, fervently.

"Thank the Lord for that. Well, that's all I can tell you. Oh—Maisie had a telephone call in her room. I gathered that she was going out as a result of the call. Now what about you?"

Roger said: "That can wait. I want to see those documents

that Hauteby was so anxious that I shouldn't see. I don't know what's in them, but there's some light in the darkness. Hauteby and Transom were in a racket together. Widdison probably wasn't. At a guess, I'd say that McFallen caught on and came to tell Transom that he wasn't going to stand for it. Transom arranged his accident. Or whoever worked with Transom did. Hauteby came here tonight to try to get the documents, of course. I suspect that what Potter was looking for was those documents in the first place." He took the envelope from his pocket, turned it over, and made sure that it was blank. "It's been handled too freely for me to worry about fingerprints."

"Open it," Mark urged.

Roger took out a penknife, and slit the top of the envelope.

They were in the study. Widdison, now in Guildford, had acted like a man struck dumb, neither protesting nor resisting. Two or three policemen were in the house, and the nurse with Mrs. Transom. Apart from that they were alone.

It was fitting, Roger thought, that they should be together then. He felt sure that the contents of the envelope would explain the whole case, the case Mark had believed was murder from the start and which had led to this fury of violence. It might not be over yet. There was the tall thin man who had escaped.

Was he Potter, forced to take a hand himself?

A thick wad of papers was inside the envelope.

"Give me one half, you go through the other," implored Mark.

"We'll read them together," said Roger. "Bring that lamp nearer."

They sat side by side at the desk, now cleaned of Wade's blood and the fragments of glass about it. The heavy curtain hung across the windows.

Roger said: "A letter on Potter's business paper, for a start. And a report of some kind attached."

The letter was simply a covering note, saying that Gabriel Potter had pleasure in enclosing the confidential report on Harringtons Limited. It was dated eighteen months earlier.

The report, an exhaustive one, said that the principal of Harringtons was a man of wide experience in rubber planting, smoking, and curing generally. He was also a research chemist, with several degrees. That his business was small and lacking in capital, but that his applications for financial help from the Government had been rejected, while he would disclose no inducement attractive enough to interest the private investor. Potter implied, however, that Harrington was working on a process for producing synthetic rubber. He did not disclose the name of his informant, but on the next sheet was a letter in a back-sloping handwriting, signed "D. Anderson," addressed to Potter, and "enclosing particulars, as arranged."

The particulars were on a single sheet of paper, containing a brief description of materials used in the process at Harrington's factory, then a very small one.

"He was selling out all right," Mark observed.

Roger nodded, and turned to the next sheet. They were in chronological order, and he imagined that they had been taken from a box in Potter's office. As he went on through other correspondence between Potter and Anderson which proved the continual exchange of information for money, the fullness of the treachery of Harrington's assistant grew more clear. Anderson had been no fool, and had only given Potter the information by instalments.

Potter's letters were models of discretion, never referring to Harrington or the business, but Anderson occasionally lapsed.

Mark said slowly:

"Anderson was putting himself in Potter's pocket, wasn't he? You can almost see Potter tightening his grip."

"I can't feel sorry for Anderson," said Roger. He flicked over several letters with no more than a casual glance, then saw one from Hauteby to Potter, asking for an interview. Potter had pencilled some notes on this, including the names of Transom and the Prendergasts. On a plain slip of paper, heavily underlined, was the statement:

"Harrington and Miss Transom meet frequently."

There followed further comments about Harrington and Garielle, records of visits from Transom without any evidence of what transpired at the meetings. Then a report, typewritten, from Potter to Transom. It gave a further opinion on Harringtons Limited and recommended that Transom put money into the company.

There were notes from a man named Conroy, Duke Conroy. Roger stopped when he came to this and looked up sharply.

"Transom said that was Harrington's true name," he said. "I—ah, here we are!"

He had found a letter from Potter to Transom. There was no doubt, it said, that the man calling himself Harrington was actually Duke Conroy, a globe-trotter with a bad reputation, wanted for murder in Rhodesia. He, Potter, was trying to find the real Harrington, and advised Transom to treat the matter confidentially until the search was concluded. Nothing was written directly, but the inference all the time was that Transom would benefit considerably if he left the hunt for the real Harrington to Potter.

"Transom shows up more badly as we go on," Mark said. "Potter knew there was no chance of him talking until he'd squeezed every penny of profit."

"I'm looking for a further mention of the Prendergasts," Roger said.

He had to wait, for next came a series of reports from Potter's clerks to the solicitor. They concerned Clay and a man named Smith. Photographs of Clay and Smith appeared, then their police records, Clay's much blacker than Smith's.

"So it was a 'Smith,'" said Mark thoughtfully, recognizing the second man as Clay's companion. "We've got Potter in the nutcracker at last."

Records of Clay's various crimes were there, with one or two notes; then they found a sinister annotation in Potter's own handwriting, concerning a hitherto mysterious attack on a bank messenger in Aldgate. Potter wrote: *Undoubtedly Clay. A violent man repressing his real nature but subject to outbursts of almost schizophrenic frenzy.*

The picture grew clearer. Clay had committed other crimes and evaded the police but not Potter. Clay became an easy victim, as did Smith. Potter had obtained a merciless grip on them, could have given the police information enough to have sent them down for ten years or even longer.

Then there were notes, some pencilled, about Duke Conroy. A newspaper clipping; a man named Harrington had been rescued off a ship torpedoed on the way to South America.

"Conroy?" Potter had pencilled.

"Harrington was in England at that time," Mark said. "It's only a year ago."

"Yes," Roger agreed. "Here's another note—*'why does Conroy call himself Harrington?'*"

That was answered a little farther on. Conroy had known Harrington in South Africa, and had taken his name after the murders in Rhodesia. There were photographs of the two men which showed some similarity, though there would never be any confusion when the two were side by side. According to some pencilled statistics, Conroy was an inch shorter than Harrington, but there was little other difference.

Next came a newspaper account of the accidental death of *Septimus Prendergast.* A note alongside it, in pencil: *Clay or who?* Then there were notes about Mark Lessing, who had been at the inquest. Nothing of importance, but the words *"Watch Lessing"* were indicative of Potter's frame of mind.

There followed accounts of Monty Prendergast's fall on the Cornish cliffs, caused by Clay and Smith, the pencilled notes inferred. Without any prior reference, there was a note:

"Claude Prendergast and Maisie Webb married."

Next Waverley Prendergast was knocked down by a car and Claude and Maisie figured more prominently. Anderson continued to call and do business, until suddenly Potter sent him a terse note: their association would be terminated. There was a record of an interview, and the comment: *"Anderson will be difficult."*

By then it grew obvious that Claude Prendergast was giving trouble. *"Not as amenable as anticipated,"* Potter wrote. *"See Harrington."* There followed notes of the interview with Harrington, the result of which was not pleasing to Potter.

It was then, some three months ago, that there was a change in the tenor of the notes and reports. Transom and Hauteby became more frequent callers. McFallen and Widdison *"knew nothing."* Then another: *"McFallen is curious, Widdison quite safe."*

Then Petrie came into the story. At an interview, Potter had told Petrie that Clay and Smith had played a part in the murder of the Prendergasts, adding that Anderson had also played a similar part, together with a hint that Transom and McFallen were involved. Potter had advised Petrie not to consult the police, but to do what he could to find evidences, saying that as soon as there was a strong enough case he himself would do that. Several interviews with Petrie were recorded, and Mark broke a long silence.

"Potter's a cold-blooded devil," he said with great vehemence. "He's been working Petrie up to these murders. There's a note, *'Petrie a first-class shot. Home Guard.'* Look, there's a note from Petrie."

The note read:

"Dear Mr. Potter,
    I must ask you to try again. I cannot rest until I know the murders of my employers are avenged. Is there no way of finding proof that will make the police act? It is destroying my nights, I am becoming a nervous wreck.
                              Eric C. Petrie."

Pencilled on the note was: *"Tell him no chance at all. Send Clay."*

Roger looked up from the letter, bleak-faced.

"The picture's forming, Mark, careful as Potter had been to dress his notes in proper legal guise. Potter got started on Petrie, then sent Clay to work him up to a fever pitch. I don't doubt that he put Petrie on the trail of Anderson first, then told him that Clay and Smith had taken part in the Prendergast murders—so he killed them too. We'll never get all the pieces to fit, but that's about what happened. Potter seems to have been planning to kill off the *Dreem directors one by one, to get Dreem* under Claude's control. From Claude to the fake Harrington, he hopes. He's going to put the man Conroy in Harrington's place." There were notes about passports and birth certificates, and: *"Clay has arranged transfer."*

Next came notes of a conference at Potter's office between Transom and Hauteby, and Potter. Behind this there was a letter from Hauteby to Transom.

"Dear Transom,

I don't trust Potter entirely, but I think we can push the thing through. Once we have financial control of Harrington's, and Harrington has gone, we're sitting pretty. I mean Conroy has gone, of course!

McFallen and Widdison are getting curious again. They know we've put money in Harrington's. Do we want them in with us? If not, I suggest a meeting, with Potter, at our place, where he turns us down, for Widdison's and McFallen's benefit. McF. is the biggest nuisance. I think he has an idea that we're trying to get rid of Harrington, and he might even suggest one day that our Harrington is really Conroy. It just won't do!!!

H.'

Transom had written back to say that he had told Potter of this new difficulty, and Potter had promised to look after it.

Mark said slowly: "He did just that. Transom and Hauteby

knew damned well that Conroy was a fake. They were nervous enough of McFallen and Widdison to want Potter to do something quickly. Potter probably put Petrie up to fixing McFallen's car while it was near Yew House, of course. I wonder if we'll ever get the minor factors?"

"I'm more concerned with getting a hard-and-fast case for a jury against Potter," said Roger grimly. "I shouldn't think it will be so difficult. I hope to God Petrie doesn't die, we need his evidence. Maisie certainly won't die, anyhow, and she'll crack under pressure. Hauteby will probably fill in a lot of details, too." He paused, glancing through the rest of the papers. There were comments about himself and Mark, suggesting, between the lines, that they were getting too near and too persistent, but nothing else until on a final sheet:

"Tell Transom that Lessing has taken these papers."

"Well I'm damned!" exclaimed Mark. "So that's why they searched my flat. Potter was playing us off against Transom and Hauteby. Transom had Potter hoodwinked very nicely, getting the papers and thus having Potter where he wanted him. The dark horse, Transom. I suppose—" he paused—"*Transom* couldn't have been putting the pressure on Potter?"

"I doubt it," Roger said. "There's no indication here that anyone is pushing him. He started off with the Prendergast interest, got on to Harrington's synthetic rubber process and saw a way of getting control of both *Dreem* and Harringtons. He had plenty of scapegoats. Transom and Hauteby for a start, Maisie at a pinch, Clay and Smith, Petrie—but all the time he was playing with fire. He must have known it when he lost these papers, discreet as they are on the surface. He grew desperate. With some reading between the lines we've got everything, except Potter in person. He's the thin man you saw, of course, and is still somewhere nearby."

"Don't forget Conroy," said Mark. "The man we haven't seen. We can't miss them this time, can we?"

"What the Guildford police miss the Home Guard should get," Roger said.

The telephone, now repaired, rang just after they had finished. Roger lifted the receiver. The excited voice of a sergeant at Guildford said:

"Mr. Lampard asked me to ring you, sir. The woman Prendergast has talked. It was *Potter* who telephoned her. *Potter* was at the house tonight."

"That's exactly what we wanted to know," said Roger. "How is Mr. Lampard?"

"He's going to Delaware in the morning," said the sergeant. "To the house, sir, and he wonders if you could meet him there at eight o'clock."

"I'll be there," promised Roger. He rang off, and explained.

"So we've got Potter," Mark said with deep satisfaction. "We've got him too tight to escape. It's the one thing I wanted above everything else."

The glow of satisfaction in his eyes made Roger feel just how important this had been to him.

"There's more good news," Roger said. "Lampard's not badly hurt. Well, it's half-past one now. If we're to get a nap we'd better bed down. Oh—damn the thing!" The telephone rang again. Mark lifted the receiver.

"That you, Lessing? Good . . . I've got your thin bloke for you, I think." It was the Home Guard officer.

"Are you serious?"

"Yes, I'm always serious." Satisfaction deepened the man's voice. "He tried to get out of a house behind you—place called The Gables. We spotted him, and he ran back for cover. I've put my company round the place, he won't get out again. You'd better bring your police pals over in a hurry."

20

POTTER IN THE NET

A burly figure materialized out of the darkness, forage cap showing at an angle against the moon-lit sky. The moon was waning; it would be gone in two or three days, and rose only in the early hours.

"You've got here at last," the Home Guard officer said.

Roger could see beyond the man's head to the outlines of The Gables; crooked outlines, with square chimney stacks rising and three pointed gables showing at the front of the house.

"Anything new?"

"Nothing. He's in there all right. I suppose," the man went on hopefully, "you just want us to stay around in case he makes another run for it? You've got plenty of police with you?"

"Three or four," said Roger. "Nothing like enough. We're going up to the house, and would like you and a couple of men in support. The men in that house will be desperate."

"Jolly good!" exclaimed the H G. "Ward—here's a job for you and Simpson." Two figures loomed out of the gloom of the surrounding trees. "Might be some stuff flying, I'm told."

"All right with me, sir," one man said.

"Oke," said the other.

"That's what I like to hear," said Mark.

There was a slight delay while Roger arranged the disposition of the four Guildford policemen whom he had collected on the way to The Gables. The quiet of the night was uncanny. The whispers of the men as orders and acceptances went to and fro added to it. There was awareness of the finality of the moment in Roger's mind. Potter was in this house, and the grounds were filled with Home Guards, so there was no chance for him to escape. Maisie had damned him. That was all that was needed on top of the evidence of the documents.

From The Gables, a clock struck clearly.

"Half-past two," said Mark. "How much longer?"

"We're about ready," Roger said.

"Three men by the back door, three by the front, three by the side," put in the lieutenant. "They're standing by in case of an attempted sortie. I'm going to the back door with one of my men and one of yours. That right?"

"Right," said Roger. "Your other man and two of mine in at the side door, and we'll take the front. If no one answers my ringing, I'll get in with Lessing and open up for you. You'd better not knock the doors about too much," he added, and the lieutenant chuckled. "Unless," Roger went on, "I send word for you to get in somehow."

They went their several ways, making little sound. Above one of the square chimney stacks a small segment of the moon showed, casting a pale light about the house and the tops of the trees. It was easy to advance in the shadows, and there was no likelihood of them being seen.

Near the front door, Mark said:

"You're not seriously going to ring the bell?"

Roger chuckled. "Why are we here alone? You're going to try to open the front door. If it's bolted as it probably will be, we'll try a window. Once we've got a start the others can move in, but we don't want them to begin the fighting."

"Thoughtful of you."

"Shut up," said Roger.

His fingers were about the automatic which Hauteby had used. It was loaded again. Mark had a gun, also loaded.

They reached the front door.

Mark used a torch for the first time, examining the lock. It promised to be easy. He worked on it, while Roger turned his back and wondered what Chatworth would say if he could see this.

Mark called softly:

"It's open."

The door was open only a fraction of an inch; a chain kept it in position. Mark tried to get his fingers on the chain but failed. He put his weight to the door, but there was no give. He shone the torch through the narrow gap.

"It's barricaded with furniture."

"I suppose we ought to have expected it," Roger said, "but I fancied Potter would try to make a defence for himself and not put up a Sydney Street. I suppose he *can't* get away?"

"You know he can't," said Mark. "I'm more interested in how many he's got with him. The man Conroy, perhaps, and the old boy Lampard mentioned—what's-his-name?—Delaroy. There might be others. Come on. They can't barricade all the windows."

They made a stealthy circle of the house.

All the windows were shuttered on the inside.

"It looks as if you'll have to use the 'open in the name of the law' gambit," Mark said.

"Go round and warn the others to be ready," Roger said. Over the front door he could see the bell-push by the light of his torch. He pressed, and then knocked on the heavy iron knocker. There was no response. He knocked again, and then shouted:

"Open in the name of the law!" He felt slightly ridiculous as the echoes of the words came back to him, and then faded into silence. He was justified now in breaking-in and using what force might be necessary, he had tried everything else.

He heard a heavy thudding on one of the shutters after a crash of breaking glass, and imagined a member of the Home Guard battering heartily with his rifle-butt.

Mark came hurrying.

"They've forced a window. Come on."

Both men raced towards the side door, and a nearby window. The officer was standing by it, with a policeman and one of his own men. Roger took a tighter grip on his gun, and climbed through the window into a darkened room. His torch shed a ghostly glare over the furniture. He barked his shin on a chair, and winced.

The door was locked.

He stood back and shattered the lock with a bullet. When he pulled at the handle the door opened. He moved very cautiously, peering into the darkened hall. He put a hand to the wall outside, searching in vain for an electric light switch. Except for faint movement of men behind him there was no sound and no sign of movement; it was as if the place was completely deserted.

He opened the door wider and stepped through, then shone his torch about the hall. Furniture was piled up against the front door, and near the light switches. There was something else; a figure lying on the carpet, between him and the switches. He put out his torch, groping for the light switches as he went round near the wall. Mark and the others stayed by the open door of the room.

The light went on.

It was dazzling enough to blind him. He narrowed his eyes against it, and squeezed back against the wall, where some of the piled furniture gave him cover from any shooting from the twisting staircase. When his eyes grew accustomed to the bright light, he looked at the figure on the carpet.

It was of an old, bald-headed man, who was dead; unless he had the secret of living with a bullet-hole in his temple.

"Delaroy," Roger murmured to himself. "I wonder why they had to kill him?" From the position of the man he judged that Delaroy had been trying to get out when he was shot. But it was Potter he wanted; he did not give a damn for anyone but Potter, and at the back of his mind there was a fear that the solicitor had managed to outwit him.

Then a man spoke from the top of the stairs.

The low ceiling hid the speaker from sight. His voice was harsh and unfamiliar, and there was a menacing note in it.

"Get out of my way, West."

Roger said quietly:

"You haven't a chance, any of you. The house is surrounded. You can't get through."

"If I can't get away from here, I can kill some of you if you don't stay put. What about *this?*"

He paused after the "this," then a stream of bullets spat out from a Thompson sub-machine gun. The staccato bark of the gun was harsh and ominous. A line was furrowed in the plaster not a yard from Roger's head.

"Wood won't keep those bullets out," the man said. "Stay where you are."

Roger said nothing.

"Listen, West. You'll send everyone in this house out, except me. Got that? You'll give the orders, in my hearing. Get a deep breath ready for a shout. Your voice has to carry."

He sent another short burst of bullets. They struck the wall near the door of the room where Mark and the others were waiting. Roger's heart was thumping. This was insanity. The man might kill him and Mark, and others, but stood no chance of getting away. He had actually acknowledged that in so many words. There seemed no reason in his attitude.

Roger made himself say:

"Conroy, you can't save Potter that way."

"Who told you I was Conroy?"

"I know who you are. Throw that gun down and give yourself up."

"And be hanged for a job I did ten years ago? I know the odds, West. This is the last chapter for me. I'll write it in red. What about giving that order?"

Roger heard a sound in the room where Mark was waiting. Conroy must have heard it, too, for he sent a spray of bullets rasping towards the door. He missed the big HG officer, who crawled out of the room on his stomach, then made a leap upwards, flinging something through the air towards the stairs. It was a hand grenade. He plunged towards the foot of the stairs with his hands about his head.

There was a blinding flash, a shout, a clattering noise, and an explosion and blast which rocked the hall. The piece of furniture behind which Roger was sheltering rocked wildly, pressing him tight against the wall. It took him a moment to recover. When he reached the hall, he saw Mark and two Home Guards going swiftly up the stairs. The Home Guard officer was already out of sight. The tommy-gun was on the staircase, where it had dropped when the hand-grenade had exploded. Just above it, sprawling head first, was a big man in grey clothes.

Roger reached him. The man was dead or unconscious, and there was an ugly wound in the side of his head. Roger stepped over him and went on. He heard heavy footsteps ahead, and wondered whether the others would find Potter before he did. He saw doors standing open, men going in and out of the rooms. Mark came from one, but did not see him.

"Where is he?" the Home Guard officer demanded. "He can't have ducked out."

"There's another floor," Mark said.

Roger thought: "I wonder if there's a cellar?" He voiced the thought, and Mark called back:

"It's being covered. You all right?"

"Yes." Roger's head was ringing from the explosion; and he was suffering from the reaction. Three times in the past three days he had been so nearly dead that he had almost resigned himself to it.

His stomach was queasy, and he had to fight for self-control. *Then he saw Potter.*

There was a cupboard on the landing, its door half-open. Potter emerged from it; long and thin, his face in shadows, his hands raised in front of him. He ducked back into the cupboard when a Home Guard appeared, then showed up again when the man went into another room. Roger stood close to the wall. Potter ran towards the landing. His face was set very bleakly, his lips a thin line, his eyes narrowed so that they looked like little slits of steel.

He went into one of the bedrooms which had already been searched by the police and Home Guard. He did not close the door behind him, and Roger reached it, fingering the automatic. There might be something else to discover yet.

Had Potter been under pressure?

Roger watched him through the crack of the door.

Potter went across the low-ceilinged room, and opened first the shutters and then the window. A cold breeze blew in, rustling the curtains, and the moonlight alone enabled Roger to see.

Potter looked out.

In the grounds someone shouted: "Watch that window! The second one along!"

Potter turned about, but did not close the window. His face was hidden, but he was muttering under his breath. He neared the door, and looked round, visible then in the light from the landing.

Footsteps approached, slowly. A shadow was thrown across the room; the shadow of a long figure with something pointed above the shape of the head; a rifle and bayonet. Potter stared towards it, then hesitated, before putting his right hand to his pocket. He drew out a gun. Roger stiffened, and crept forward. Potter approached the door very slowly, and then there was a sound at the window and a man's head and shoulders appeared.

Potter swung round.

He raised his gun. The man in the window was a clear target, unable to save himself. Roger moved, swift and soft, and struck

Potter's gun-arm upwards. The report and the flash of a shot came almost simultaneously. Potter swung round. Roger knocked the gun out of his hand, pointed his own gun towards Potter's stomach and stared into the cold grey eyes.

21

PRESSURE

Potter made a quick movement, to free himself.

Roger drew back and shot out his left fist, striking Potter on the side of the chin. The blow sent the man staggering. Hurried footsteps sounded outside and on the stairs as Potter fell back.

"It's all right," Roger said. "Switch on the light, will you?"

"Can't," a man said. "The black-out's not up."

"Soon fix that," said a man by the window.

How unimportant everyday things seemed. Here was Potter, reeling under the blow, disarmed, and helpless. When the light came on, he was leaning against the wall, fingering his chin. He looked a very old man, and his expression was dazed—not venomous or malignant, just dazed.

"This the man you want?" asked a Home Guard.

"That's the man," said Roger. He put a hand to his pocket for handcuffs. Potter stared, then slowly extended his hands. The handcuffs clicked as Mark rushed into the room.

"You've got him! I don't believe it."

"You can believe it," said Roger. "Have you found anyone else?"

"Not a soul except the two fellows you've seen. Where was he?"

"In a linen cupboard," said Roger. "It was as easy as kiss your hand." He looked into Potter's eyes, and said: "Now then, Potter, you're coming with me."

Potter said with an effort: "I have nothing to say. Nothing to say."

. . . .

Roger sat in Lampard's office at Guildford. The effect of Hauteby's kick had not entirely faded, for Lampard looked very pale especially about the lips and the eyes. But he smiled once or twice during the story, and Mark's asides.

In front of him were the documents.

"So we have the complete case, West," he said. "It's a time for mutual congratulations."

"Yes, I suppose so." Roger seemed doubtful.

"Only suppose?" Lampard raised his eyebrows. "Surely you don't expect more?"

"I don't know what to think," said Roger. "It must be the reaction. I didn't really believe we'd get Potter so completely. He must have been crazy to try to fight it out."

"He was simply desperate, and like most desperate animals clung to hope as long as he could," reasoned Lampard. "The man Conroy was much the same. He knew that once we caught him, he would be finished. He preferred to die fighting. He is dead, by the way, but he admitted killing Delaroy, who was Potter's sleeping partner in all this business. Potter had gathered together a gallery of rogues and a complexity of motives bigger than anything I've ever known. You can see that."

"There are some things I don't see," Roger said. "Potter came into the open when he could have made a fortune out of *Dreem*. That's why it doesn't make sense. I can't believe he would have gone in for wholesale murder unless he was under pressure he couldn't resist. Someone had influence over Potter as he had over Clay and the other crooks."

Lampard shrugged. "Stubbornness over the Prendergast 'accidents' certainly brought results," he admitted. There was a curious tone in his voice, almost as if he was keeping something back. He seemed glad when the telephone rang: "This will be your call to the Yard."

Roger leaned over the desk and lifted the receiver. A girl said: "Your personal call to Mayfair. Hold on please. Hallo, Mayfair 00121. You're through." A deep voice said: "'Hallo, West, what's all this about?" It was Chatworth.

Roger drew a deep breath.

"I thought I'd better ring you at your home, sir, with stop press news. We've got Potter for murder and conspiracy to murder, and probably on about a dozen other counts."

The Assistant Commissioner made a sound over the wires, a cross between a cluck and a chortle.

"I'm very glad to hear it. Very glad indeed. Is it too much to hope that he has talked?" Chatworth contrived to make it sound as if Roger should have forced Potter to talk his head off.

"He hasn't yet."

"Well, keep at him. Don't spoil a good job. I understood you to imply that Potter will be convicted of murder, but there are others, West. There are always others! Have you explored every other possibility? That little idea you had, for instance, that someone was—what was the phrase?—pushing Potter."

"I've tried it," said Roger. "I still believe there is someone, sir, but there's no evidence. No one who has talked, and that includes Hauteby, Maisie Prendergast, and Petrie, appears to have any doubt that Potter was working for himself. I think they would have named the man if they knew him or said if they'd suspected anyone."

"Yes," conceded Chatworth. "Yes, I suppose so. I don't want to throw cold water over your achievement, West, but *do* try all you can. Ring me later. Meanwhile congratulations on what you've done so far."

Roger heard the receiver click at the other end, and replaced his own slowly. Lampard and Mark were on edge, and Mark said explosively:

"The old basket can't want anything more."

"He wants exactly what I want," said Roger. "I wish he would learn to talk without a sting in every other sentence." He looked moodily at Lampard. "He's bitten by my bug. That someone's behind Potter."

"Supposing you come home with me and have some breakfast," Lampard suggested. "You need a rest, too."

Lampard lived near the station, and introduced his wife, who looked as young as Janet and was nearly as pleasing on the eye. She had been warned to expect Mark and Roger, and breakfast was sizzling on a hot plate. Lampard threw off the cold, formal manner and became positively human, although the first time Mark heard him call his wife "darling" Mark nearly choked.

Little was said about the case until they had left the house and were walking back to the station.

Lampard said conversationally:

"The report on Harrington is satisfactory, I'm glad to say. Miss Transom—I'm sorry, Mrs. Harrington—had been persuaded to go back to Yew House. Petrie had made a full statement, as you know. The story in those documents is clearly corroborated. Mrs. Prendergast will live to hang, but I think Petrie will escape that, he won't live for a trial. I feel rather glad, don't you, Mr. Lessing?"

"Yes," said Mark.

"So we have everything explained and everything pigeonholed." Lampard smiled. "Except for the one remaining obsession, of course! Hallo, here is Dr. Tenby."

The doctor was approaching the station from the opposite direction. He stopped at a sight of the trio, and smiled a little grimly. "You were nearly late, Lampard." He nodded to the others. "I've checked it."

"Checked what?" asked Roger.

"Do you know, I have an uncomfortable feeling that Lampard is going to put something across us," said Mark. He sent a sideways glance to Lampard, whose lips were curving. Tenby gave a short laugh, then compressed his lips. They filed into Lampard's office. Tenby took a small bottle from his waistcoat pocket, and handed it to Lampard.

"That's it," he said. "Barbitone tablets."

Roger said: "Barbitone?"

"One of the hypnotic drugs," said Tenby.

"Yes, I know what barbitone is," said Roger, with a touch of impatience. "Three or four tablets would put a man out, and if you didn't know what was causing the collapse you'd think he was going to die." He stared at Tenby as he went on: "Barbitone would have made Claude Prendergast look as ill as he was, and could make him behave as he did."

"That's right," said Tenby. "It did, too. This was found in his luggage by Lampard. An unmarked bottle, but barbitone all right."

"Do you know where he got it from?"

"I do," Lampard said, almost smugly. "I do indeed. From the Red Cross room at Harrington's factory. There is a selection of drugs there, and this has an identifying mark. See?" He pointed to a red H in a circle. "That's stamped on all the bottles and tins at the factory, in red. You know the truth, West, don't you?"

Roger felt very wary.

"No. Do you?"

"Our man is Harrington," Lampard said, making no attempt to hide his satisfaction and his elation. "He fits in everywhere— opportunity, motive—to get control of *Dreem* and so have all the finance he needed for his synthetic rubber, personal hatred of *Dreem* directors, and access to their association with Potter. Well? Don't you agree?"

"Harrington," breathed Mark.

"Harrington," echoed Roger. "I wonder. Dr. Tenby, as this drug was in Claude Prendergast's things, he could have taken it himself, couldn't he?"

"Well, yes, but—"

"What difference does it make?" demanded Lampard. "He could have been coerced into taking it by his wife, or even given a dose by her on Harrington's orders. Mrs. Prendergast's demonstration of hostility to Harrington could have been feigned, to give us the impression that she hated him."

"Oh, undoubtedly," Roger said. "Mark, could Claude have taken this stuff when you first went to Delaware—a little while before he was taken ill?"

Mark said: "Yes, I left him alone once or twice."

"*Claude*," breathed Roger.

"I have a feeling that you are trying to rob me of my thunder," said Lampard. "If we talk to Harrington—"

"Dr. Tenby knows Claude Prendergast pretty well. When Claude collapsed he looked for evidence of a drug, of course. We now know for certain what it was," said Roger. "Didn't we all think he was the last of the Prendergast victims? But if he dosed himself with a drug so as to seem a victim, that could answer most of our questions. I always wanted to know why Claude should take such an interest in *Dreem*, why he rounded on his wife as he did."

Lampard said slowly: "I admit it's a point."

"I'm asking myself what he would have done had he known what his wife and Potter were planning," went on Roger. "Obviously he would come out far better if he could direct operations without being suspected. Couldn't he? How often do we suspect a 'victim'? I've never been able to believe that Potter was acting voluntarily. But Claude Prendergast, having full knowledge of the situation, could easily have given instructions." Roger tried not to show his excitement. "Potter would have been compelled to act as he did and to make the arrangements, because Claude could incriminate him so easily. Potter needn't have known who was exerting the influence." Roger gave a chuckle, remarkably like one of Chatworth's.

Lampard said: "Claude Prendergast fits in better than Harrington, but how did Claude get this poison?"

"If Anderson were alive we could ask him," said Roger drily. "It looks as if Claude learned of the plot against Harrington and used that to make Potter get rid of the Prendergasts. Think of his position if he then planned to be rid also of the other directors and remain in sole control of *Dreem*."

"Shall we go and see him?" Lampard asked. "I confess I would rather you were right."

He drove them all to Delaware. Roger and Mark sat in the tonneau in silence. Tenby and Lampard talked animatedly about Prendergast. Neither of them had liked Claude, and both believed he was much more astute than he had made out.

As they were climbing from the car, Lampard asked:

"Do you think getting control of *Dreem* and Harringtons was the main motive?"

Roger closed the door with a bang.

"I doubt it," he said. "I think the prior motive, the cause for all of this, was in Claude Prendergast's hatred for his family, which disliked his ways and his habits. He was virtually thrown out with a small allowance, and it rankled. From the time of Septimus Prendergast's death, Claude's been a possibility, but until I knew he could have drugged himself—"

He didn't finish.

Claude was in his room, in a gaudy dressing-gown. He was pale, and his saucer-like eyes were very wide open yet tired. His hair was plastered over his bumpy head, and in his manner was a hint of the nervousness which he often showed vividly.

"Hallo, hallo," he said with forced geniality. "Hope you gentlemen have come with the news that it's all over. My God, I don't feel safe even now. Eh?"

This was Lampard's moment. Roger watched him, while Mark straddled a chair and Tenby stood by the door.

"Yes, it's all over," said Lampard. "Mr. Prendergast, as you know, your wife is under arrest and in hospital."

"I just can't believe Maisie'd do anything so wicked," said Claude. "I knew she was a bit of a spitfire, but—do—do you think she tried to put *me* away?"

"No, I don't," said Lampard. "But she has told a peculiar story, Mr. Prendergast. Do you remember reporting to Inspector West that she often talked in her sleep?"

Claude said: "What about it?"

Lampard smiled. "So do you," he said.

After a few seconds, when the shock struck, Claude wilted. He began to quiver. Any doubts in Roger's mind were swept aside at his change of expression, and the positive malignance in his eyes.

"The bitch!" he cried. "She's been lying to you! What's she been saying?"

"Amongst other things, we want to know why you drugged yourself with this," said Lampard. Dr. Tenby produced the bottle like a rabbit out of a hat. "Why did you?"

"It's a damnable lie! My wife's trying to drag me down with her. She—"

"Supposing you keep your opinion of your wife to yourself?" Lampard said coldly. "Mr. Lessing, you remember seeing Prendergast take the tablets? Out of that bottle?" He pointed to Tenby and stepped between Claude and Mark, so that the former could not see Mark's temporary expression of surprise.

Mark had some of his composure back.

"I did."

"If a man wants to drug himself to get some sleep—" began Claude. Then he stopped short as if realizing that any kind of admission might be damning. He drew back, his lips working.

"Claude Prendergast, I am charging you with being concerned with the murders of your grandfather, your father, and your brother," Lampard said. "Anything you say may be taken in evidence against you." He took a pair of handcuffs from his pocket, and took a step forward.

"No!" shrieked Claude. "You can't know that. You can't *do* that! They died by accident. Anyhow, Potter did it, Potter arranged it all."

"You will have a chance to prove that in court," Lampard said.

Claude turned and ran towards the window. Roger and Mark were there ahead of him, holding his writhing figure while he mouthed and shouted and blasphemed; and damned himself.

"If Potter were handling this case," Roger said a little later, "he'd get away with an insanity plea. We couldn't have made a thorough job of Prendergast if you hadn't handled Potter, Mark."

Lampard chuckled.

"Congratulations, Mr. Lessing," he said.

"I'll buy you both a dinner when we've got this case over," Roger said. "Meanwhile I'm going to report to the AC."

. . . .

A large tabby cat strolled thoughtfully into the lounge of the West's Bell Street house. It peered at Janet and Roger, and Mark, and then at the fireplace. There was no fire, for it was in the middle of a heatwave which made the Assize Court hot and stuffy for the five days of Claude's and Potter's trial. The cat jumped out of the window at a single bound. They watched it strolling into the street, disdainful of passers by.

Roger rubbed his chin.

"When I first fell over Lamp *alias* Quisling, I cursed him," he said. "Bless his heart, if he only knew what he had started. Well, it's all over at last. All the convictions we wanted. Harrington gave his evidence well this afternoon," he added thoughtfully. "He tells me he's buying up *Dreem* shares as fast as they come on the market. He'll be one of our industrial giants of the future." He looked at the window as the cat jumped into the room again, and chuckled. "Hallo, Lamp," he said. "Aren't they any more sociable out of doors?"

"Why the Lamp?" asked Mark. "I haven't heard this one. The cat that lighted the way, I suppose?"

"Certainly not," said Roger. "The name's short for Lampard, who turned out to be much nicer than he seemed at first." He watched the tabby jump on to Janet's knee. Janet buried her fingers in his fur.

Mark coughed.

"This is no place for me," he said. He crossed to the piano, his fingers beginning to caress the keys. He was playing a haunting thing from Brahms when two people entered the garden—a man and a woman.

Janet jumped up. "Good gracious, the Harringtons! Open the door, darling, and give me a chance to tidy my hair." She put her fingers to her hair to straighten it, tucking and coiling.

Garielle and Harrington came in.

"We simply want to give these to Mark," said Harrington, and handed Mark a neatly-wrapped package.

"We've decided to open Delaware again," declared Garielle. "Mrs. West, you will come for a long weekend as soon as the Yard lets your husband off, won't you?"

"We'd love to," said Janet.

"Love to," echoed Roger.

"Me too?" asked Mark, cutting the string, then opening the cardboard box inside the paper. There was a packing of straw, and his fingers explored until he drew out one of the le Fleur masks from Harrington's flat, then a second, then a third.

"Just in case you decide to go back to collecting china," said Harrington. "By the way, give me Pep Morgan's address, will you? The man with the big nose, I mean. I can't risk offering you people a wad of *Dreem* shares, but Morgan deserves to be in on the ground floor. Garry, we'll have to hurry or we'll miss that train."